I0602032

DARK HEARTS

TALES OF TWISTED LOVE

Edited by A.R. Ward

Illustrated by Ashley Van Elswyk

Dark Hearts

A Ghost Orchid Press Anthology

Copyright © 2021 Ghost Orchid Press

First published in Great Britain 2021 by Ghost Orchid Press

The authors of the individual stories retain the copyright of the works featured in this anthology.

This is a work of fiction. Names, characters, places, and incidents either are the product of the author's imagination or are used fictitiously. Any resemblance to actual persons, living or dead, events, or locales is entirely coincidental.

All rights reserved. No part of this production may be reproduced, stored in a retrieval system, or transmitted in any form or by any means, electronic, recording, mechanical, photocopying or otherwise without the prior written permission of the publisher and copyright owner.

ISBN (paperback): 978-1-8383915-2-2

ISBN (e-book): 978-1-8383915-3-9

Cover illustration © GrandeDuc via. Shutterstock

Book formatting and cover design by Claire Saag

Interior illustrations © Ashley Van Elswyk

"Have you ever been in love? Horrible, isn't it?"

—Neil Gaiman, *The Kindly Ones*

CONTENTS

FOREWORD

Heartbreak. Obsession. Grief. Jealousy. Love can turn tainted, even cruel. *Dark Hearts: Tales of Twisted Love* is a collection of twenty horrifying stories about love turned sinister. These established and debut authors aren't afraid to examine difficult subjects, or dip into the darker recesses of human emotion, in stories that are original, unexpected, and thought-provoking.

The collection begins with a woman who attempts to design her ideal mate and ends with an unrequited love that lasts beyond the grave. In between, you'll find breakups, stalkers, abusive husbands, and cult followers. You will discover macabre taxidermists, obsessive lepidopterists, and vengeful ghosts. Queer love stories abound, and the volume is not restricted to romantic love, either.

One thing is for certain: after reading these stories you'll find yourself looking at love in an entirely different light.

I hope you enjoy the read.

A.R. Ward

DEARLY DEVOTED
Kelly Piner

Kay Sims hopped out of bed on Monday morning and thumbed through her wardrobe, looking for the just the right outfit. She showered and took extra care with her hair and makeup and then donned a sleek red wool sheath. She accessorized with a single strand of pearls, black pumps, and a black clutch—simple yet sophisticated. She twirled once before the mirror and then grabbed her keys, certain that she had chosen well for her first meeting with the CEO of Made to Order.

After years of disappointment, she had wondered if she would ever find true love. And then a year ago, the ad had leapt off the page: **Made to Order.** Find perfect, everlasting love—guaranteed! The first business of its kind, Made to Order specialised in creating the perfect mate. Clients specified physical traits such as height, eye and hair colour, and even some personality characteristics. Never again would she be relegated to the back burner by a man, treated as nothing more than a stick of old furniture.

Believing it too good to be true, Kay had waited months before making the call. Much like buying a new model car, best to wait until all the bugs had been worked out, she thought. She revelled in the prospects. No more lonely nights. No more chaos or conflict. When she found the courage to place her order, she felt confident that Made to Order would do its best for her. She had even paid extra for the fine-tuning that would have her mate attentively listen to her at the end of the day. For $5,000 more, she had ensured that he would be totally devoted to her and never forget her birthday or holidays.

Two months ago, during her first visit to the Made to Order facility, Kay had spent three hours watching video testimonials from happy couples. One woman in particular stood out. Dora had divorced two cheating husbands and had also ordered a partner who would be totally devoted. Devotion was the most sought after quality requested by women, a voice-over informed Kay, as Dora's mechanical mate, Robert, gazed attentively at her throughout the video. To anyone observing, Robert only had eyes for Dora. The image sent tingles down Kay's spine. To think that soon her new mate could be gazing at her in the same heart-warming manner.

At 8:30 a.m., Kay wheeled her BMW up to the stately old brick building situated in a heavily wooded area surrounded by vibrant orange autumn leaves. She inhaled the crisp October air and looked around at the stone paths and manicured grass that reminded her of her old Ivy League campus. Inside, an assistant named Sage showed her into the waiting area. Kay took deep breaths to quiet the fluttering within her chest.

A little before nine, the CEO strode into the waiting room. In his mid-fifties, with salt and pepper hair and piercing eyes as black as onyx, he warmly embraced Kay's hand. "Ms Sims? Maurice Tyler. Follow me."

He ushered her into his office and as they spoke over his desk, he never broke his gaze, making Kay feel like his most important client. Yes, he confidently assured her, he had reviewed her application. "In fact, the technicians are fine-tuning your Laurence even as we speak. We've had great luck producing men who are totally devoted," he proudly professed. "I see no problem at all in meeting all of your specifications."

Kay fiddled with the hem of her dress.

As if sensing her nervousness, he leaned in. "Your perfect mate will be ready by noon and will be fully activated when he leaves the facility. You'll only need to introduce yourself. Your voice, photo, and preferences will be imprinted on his memory chip. Do you have any questions?"

Kay had a million questions, but couldn't think of a single one at that moment. Her head reeled. She'd have plenty of time for questions later.

At the conclusion of the meeting, Mr Tyler walked Kay to the front lobby and reiterated his happiness for her. "You'll never be sorry," he assured her. "Sage will escort you to the reception area, where I will personally deliver Laurence."

Kay clutched at her throat, unable to speak at first. "I don't know what to say. I've never been so nervous and excited."

"This is a big day," he said. "Just relax." He motioned to Sage and then disappeared through a back door.

Plush carpeting and cushioned armchairs with squishy pillows decorated the reception room, where a carafe of coffee and a silver platter of Danish had been placed on a modern round oak table. Soft flute music played through overhead speakers, and the swooshing noise of a nearby portable waterfall lulled Kay into a deep state of relaxation.

Sage motioned to the table. "Help yourself to the refreshments and relax. When the buzzer sounds at the rear door, please open it and greet your mate." She smiled and left Kay alone.

Kay poured herself coffee and sipped it to calm her nerves. But how could she relax when soon she'd come face-to-face with her lifelong mate? She checked and rechecked her hair and makeup in the deco mirror. She paced back and forth, periodically peeking out the blinds, and at noon, two car doors slammed outside, followed by footsteps on the walkway. The buzzer sounded.

Kay took a deep breath, placed her shaky hand on the doorknob and flung it open. She gasped as she came face to face with Laurence, who exceeded all her expectations. A combination of rugged handsomeness combined with old Hollywood charm and sophistication, he stood five feet ten inches tall with a thick mop of blonde hair. His steel-blue eyes locked with hers. Tiny crow's feet appeared at the corners of his eyes when he smiled, and he appeared to be in his early fifties. Since her mate would never age, she had specified he be ten to twelve years her senior. Immaculately dressed in a crisp white shirt, blue tie, and grey dress slacks, he wore top of the line Italian loafers. In his right hand, he grasped a bouquet of yellow roses, her favourite. Kay stood speechless until Mr Tyler broke the spell.

"Kay, I introduce you to Laurence."

Laurence presented Kay the roses, took her left hand, and seductively kissed her knuckles, sending chills down her spine. His touch felt so human. He stepped inside the foyer, his eyes still on Kay.

"I am so honoured to finally meet you," he professed, with a proper British accent.

Kay's cheeks burned. A miracle had just walked into her life. What wonders awaited her with the most perfect specimen of a man she had ever met?

Mr Tyler motioned to the oak table in the corner of the room. "Let's have refreshments and get acquainted."

A perfect gentleman, Laurence pulled Kay's chair. She poured coffee as Mr Tyler chattered something about instructions, but she didn't hear half of what he said. Practically giddy, she yearned to be alone with Laurence.

Twenty minutes later, Mr Tyler walked the new couple to the front entrance. He took Kay's hand in his. "Don't hesitate to call with any questions or concerns," he said, and then left Kay alone with Laurence for the first time.

As nervous as a teenager on her first date, Kay couldn't help but wonder if she and Laurence would appear in their own video in a few months, professing their love for one another. In the parking lot, Laurence opened her car door, and Kay slid behind the wheel and placed her trembling foot on the gas pedal. With Laurence by her side, she chattered and drove aimlessly around town before giving him a tour of her neighbourhood. She stopped at a tiny café where colourful flower boxes adorned the front entrance. Female patrons shot Kay envious looks. Did they know he was a robot?

Laurence cupped her left hand in his as she sipped her cappuccino. His intoxicating cologne wafted in the air, and he hung onto her every word.

Back at her house, Kay turned to him and asked, "What would you like to do?" just as if he were a real person and not a robot.

"You decide," Laurence said.

You decide—music to her ears after years of power struggles with men. She took his hand and strolled with him through the house to show him each room. He nodded in approval and made appropriate comments during the tour.

And then he spun her around to face him. "We can spend summer evenings on the deck overlooking the garden." He seemed to intuitively know her preferences, as if he could read her mind.

Later that evening, Kay made a romantic candlelit dinner. She had forgotten that Laurence was a machine who could not eat. Instead, he admired her as she munched on a Caesar salad, and afterwards, he helped with the dishes and then they watched Kay's favourite movie, a romantic classic. No more moaning or groaning about her movies; no more apologies about her decisions, since Laurence appeared intrigued by all her choices. Had she died and gone to heaven?

When the credits rolled at the end of the movie, Laurence squeezed her hand, and Kay's heart fluttered. He caressed her shoulder and said, "I'll stay in the guest room for the time being until we really get to know each other. In fact, let's wait until after our ceremony before spending the night together."

Kay felt as if she were starring in her own late-night movie with a proper, old-fashioned courtship and wedding night, and this feeling only continued the next day. She had taken the week off work so she and Laurence could get to know one another, but what about when she returned to work? She regularly put in over sixty hours a week at the PR firm. How would Laurence fill so many empty hours? Then she remembered that robots were not subject to such petty human emotions as boredom and loneliness.

The days with Laurence felt like minutes, with each day proving more magnificent than the last. Whatever Kay wanted, Laurence obliged. Having never before been subjected to such royal treatment, Kay forgot that Laurence had been programmed to please her.

On Saturday evening, they stood in front of the fireplace in Kay's living room—her in a pink satin cocktail dress, and him in a grey suit she had purchased for him. With no need for an audience, they privately exchanged personalised vows of lifetime commitment.

Laurence gazed lovingly at Kay as they exchanged vows, and then he slid a simple gold band onto her finger. Robot or no robot, Kay knew that she had struck gold. She may have only known Laurence for a week, but she could not imagine life without him.

On this, her wedding night, Kay wore her pink French nightgown, and Laurence lived up to the fantasy. He incorporated the best qualities of her past lovers, all rolled up into one man. She had never felt such love for any mortal man. She would never again have to be "out there," playing the dating game. Laurence had cost her a small fortune and had used up a sizable portion of her inheritance, but Kay didn't mind. What good was money if she ended up dying alone and isolated?

On Monday morning, Kay clasped Laurence's hands in hers. "I can't stand the thought of leaving you, but I have to return to work. What will you do with yourself?"

Laurence smiled. "Don't you worry. I'll read some of your favourite books, and we can discuss them over the weekend." At the front door, he passionately kissed her. "I already miss you," he said, as he wrapped a sweater around her shoulders and walked her to her car.

Kay drove down her tree-lined street in her black convertible. She shook her head at the thought that scores of women had settled for mere mortals, never knowing true love or devotion.

Later in the day, Laurence's phone call broke the chaos of Kay's first day back at the office. "How is your day going, darling?"

"You wouldn't believe the mess waiting for me here," she said.

"Well, I have a surprise for you later tonight." He wouldn't give even a hint. "You'll just have to wait and see for yourself."

Just past seven, Kay arrived home to the aroma of a savoury roast with rosemary simmering in the oven. Rose petals lined a path to the ensuite where Laurence had drawn a warm bath. Her favourite champagne chilled in a silver bucket. As she relaxed in the bubble bath, he put the final touches on dinner and kept her champagne flute filled, his entire existence devoted to her happiness.

Kay couldn't wait until Mr Tyler called for her initial progress report. But with an unusually heavy schedule that first week back at the PR firm, she worked late several evenings. On Thursday she didn't arrive home until almost ten, and Laurence met her at the door, looking harried and out of breath. "I've been worried," he said.

"That's so sweet," she said, her fingers at her throat. She hadn't realised that a robot could "worry," but she had paid extra to fine tune those traits she desired, and this included having a mate worry about her.

She kissed Laurence's cheek as he reheated her meal and sat close to her at the dinner table, soaking up every word as she described her day.

But the next day, when Kay's cell flashed Laurence's name during an important lunch meeting, she shoved the phone back into her purse. This caused Laurence to call twice more. When she finally returned his call around two that afternoon, chilliness had overtaken the concerned, charming man she'd kissed goodbye earlier that morning.

"I've been worried," Laurence said, his voice accusing.

"I'm sorry, darling, but I've been in meetings all day." When he only breathed into the telephone, she asked, "Laurence, are you there?" She wondered if they had a bad connection.

"I'm here," he said, his tone distant and hurt. "I'll see you this evening. What time can I expect you?"

A knot gripped Kay's chest. She actually felt guilty about working and not being at home. She pressed her hand to her forehead. The relationship was new. They were still getting used to each other. No cause for concern, she reminded herself. It would take time. After all, no relationship is all wine and roses.

She arrived home around seven that evening to an empty house, with Laurence nowhere to be found. He couldn't drive and had no car, even if he could. She paced the floor and waited and was even thinking of calling Mr Tyler when Laurence strolled in around eight thirty. Without saying a word, without looking at Kay or acknowledging her in any way, he walked straight to the bedroom and hung up his coat.

"Where were you?" Kay asked, a hint of panic in her voice.

"Doesn't feel so good when the shoe is on the other foot, does it?" he shot back.

Kay's blood ran cold. Had he actually done this on purpose, to be vengeful, as payback for her long hours at the office? But how could a robot be vengeful? And why had his total devotion suddenly turned to possessiveness? She would phone Mr Tyler first thing Saturday morning with her concerns. Had this happened with any of the other robots? If so, what would they do about it?

Exhausted from her long week at work, Kay tried to salvage the evening by apologising, and suggested that they go out to dinner. Laurence reluctantly agreed, but he remained stiff and distant throughout the evening, as Kay attempted small talk.

That evening, no bubble bath or rose petals awaited her, and Laurence slept with his back to her. Even from her side of the bed, Kay sensed his anger. How had her dream man so quickly turned into a control freak with a mind of his own?

At the first hint of daylight, Kay slipped out of bed and dressed in the bathroom, but when she opened the door, Laurence sat up in bed and met her gaze.

"Where are you going so early?"

Attempting to contain the panic rising in her chest, she said, "We're out of coffee. I'm running to the corner market."

Laurence stared right through her. "I'll dress and go with you."

Certain he now suspected her intention, Kay couldn't risk calling Mr Tyler from the house lest Laurence overhear. She felt trapped—a prisoner in her own home.

"I'll just be a minute," she said. "Why don't you start breakfast?"

Without giving him a chance to respond, she grabbed her keys and darted to her car. As she pulled out of the driveway, she dialled Mr Tyler's number. When he didn't answer, she left a panicked message, then worried that she had made a mistake asking him to call back, as Laurence would overhear any phone conversation she might have. She drove in circles, thinking, until her phone rang. Her heart sank when she saw Laurence's number.

"When will you be home? What do you want for breakfast?" he asked.

"I didn't realise I needed gas. I'll be home directly." Kay ended the call to free her phone, and almost immediately, Mr Tyler returned her call.

Mr Tyler chuckled when he heard Kay's concerns. "I wouldn't make too much of it," he said, dismissively.

"How can you say that? He's acting like a complete stranger. Have you had anything like this happen before?"

He paused and then admitted, "A couple of models had to be fine-tuned initially, but nothing like what you're suggesting. Don't worry. Everything will be fine, but please call if things take a turn for the worse."

Uncomforted and feeling trivialised, Kay returned home, where Laurence sat in the sunroom looking out the window. He stood when he saw her and spoke excitedly. "I've planned our whole day. We'll start with breakfast at a new country inn I read about, followed by a long stroll along the river, an afternoon picnic, and then a movie. We'll end the day with a visit to the new bookstore in Sherrington."

Kay's head reeled, but she forced a smile. "I thought we'd spend a quiet day at home, you know, movies and popcorn?"

Laurence looked disappointed. "What's wrong? Don't you love me anymore?"

Kay had asked to be his number one priority, but this...? The look in his eyes was one of an angry dog right before it attacked. She wanted to run away, but where would she go? Laurence never let her out of his sight.

She kept replaying Mr Tyler's comments that this was no cause for concern. After all, Laurence was a robot who might be subject to strange looks and behaviours. What did she expect? He was a machine.

In an attempt to placate him, Kay spoke softly. "Of course I still love you, but I'm tired and prefer a quiet day at home with you."

He accepted her request and made popcorn and held Kay's hand during the movie, and the day passed without further incident. He told Kay to relax and even made her favourite dinner—filet mignon with grilled asparagus and creamy mashed potatoes. But after dinner, just as Kay let go her previous concerns, Laurence started in again with the questions. This time the exchange bordered on an interrogation.

"How late will you be coming home next week?" he asked, his tone once more angry.

"I don't know. Why do you ask?" Kay said, trying to get the upper hand.

"I don't appreciate being left alone all day and half the night."

That same uneasy feeling washed over her—as if she were a prisoner in her own home. But attempting to sound confident and in charge, she said, "I'll be gone as long as I need to be gone, and you'll just have to get used to it."

Laurence's eyes glazed over, and he shook his head. "No. I won't stand for being left alone. This isn't what I bargained for." His voice had grown loud.

Kay struggled to hide her fear. She had always heard that about dogs—don't show fear. Where was that devoted, loving man she had ordered—someone whose only duty was to meet her needs? He was a worse hassle than her ex. At least her ex-husband Rich had ignored her.

"You're here for me," Kay yelled. "It's not the other way around." She tried walking away, but Laurence grabbed her arm, sinking his robotic fingers deeply into her flesh.

She winced. "Laurence, let go. You're hurting me."

But he looked right through her with the same glazed expression. And then, as if someone had flipped a switch, he let go. "I'm so sorry, Kay. I never meant to hurt you. I don't know what got into me." He checked her arm and asked what he could do for her.

Kay's arm throbbed. A welt had formed. She pulled away from him and rubbed the injured arm. Tears filled her eyes, and her voice cracked when she spoke. "Why did you do that? What's happened to you?"

He shook his head. "I don't know. I don't know." He stepped closer and put his palms up in the air. "I can promise you it will never happen again."

No way could Mr Tyler dismiss this report. Something was wrong with Laurence's programming. It had to be corrected. But what if it couldn't be altered? It had never occurred to her to ask if she would be compensated if things did not turn out well. A warranty on a mate—it sounded absurd. If she returned him, she'd be out of her inheritance and back to square one. There had to be something Mr Tyler could do to correct the problem, if she called again and impressed upon him the urgency of the situation. So she suggested to Laurence that they go to bed and have a fresh start Sunday morning.

She dozed only a few hours that night, fearful of Laurence's next move, and early Sunday morning, she crept into the guest bathroom to phone Mr Tyler. She left the water running, so Laurence wouldn't overhear, and when Mr Tyler didn't answer, she left an urgent message stressing the seriousness of the situation. He had to believe her now. She stayed in the bathroom another twenty minutes relaxing in the tub, but when Mr Tyler still had not called, she returned to the living room.

Laurence met her with suspicion. He had made breakfast and asked her to have a seat. "So who were you calling?" he asked.

Kay feared that he already knew. She figured she had to fight fire with fire and angrily shot back. "I won't be interrogated in my own home."

Laurence yanked out a chair and slammed it hard against the tile floor and slumped into it. He put his knuckles to his mouth and had a faraway look, as if plotting.

Kay picked at her omelette and home fries.

Afterwards, Laurence tossed the breakfast dishes into the dishwasher, all the time ignoring her. She considered having him picked up by Made to Order on Monday, but how would she get out of his sight long enough to arrange that? Plus, what if the company refused to come and get him? What if she were stuck with him for life? The thought left her feeling weak.

Worse yet, Laurence seemed to instinctively sense her next move and next thought and stayed at her side all day. Her car keys, which she always kept in the wicker basket near the front door, had vanished. As the hours ticked by, Mr Tyler never returned her call.

That evening during dinner, Laurence stepped up his interrogation. "I don't want you leaving tomorrow." He confessed in a panicked, pathetic tone, "I'm afraid you won't return."

Struggling to project a carefree attitude, Kay assured him that she wanted nothing more than to return to him at the end of the day. "Laurence, I dream about you all day and can't wait to be with you at night."

But he shook his head and held his hand up to silence her, as if he didn't buy it. And when he spoke, his voiced dragged, like a dying battery. "That's not true. You want to get rid of me. Don't say it's not true, because I know it is."

"If you're so concerned, why don't we go together tomorrow and see Mr Tyler?" Her voice broke. "He can convince you of my undying commitment."

But Laurence defiantly shook his head. "I won't let that happen. No way will I let you and Mr Tyler take me away and destroy me." He spoke in a deliberate, measured tone, his lip curled with disgust. "You women are never satisfied. You say one thing and mean another. You wanted a man who was totally devoted, but you're not happy. Nothing is ever good enough for you women." He waved his arms in the air, as if terribly deceived.

Kay sat in silence. Her stomach hurt and soon she felt uneasy, like she'd been cast into some kind of fog. When she tried to speak, her words slurred, and she felt faint. She rose from her chair, but teetered back and forth. She only vaguely noticed when Laurence carried her into the bedroom.

Groggy and disoriented, Kay had no concept of time or place. How long she had been asleep, and where was she anyway? Lifting a hand to her head, where she felt excruciating pain, she learned that her eyes were heavily bandaged and felt as though sand had been poured into them. She cried out for help and clawed at the bandages.

Then Laurence's voice reassured her. "Don't worry, Kay. It'll be alright. I'm right here by your side." He gently caressed her hand.

Tears welled up inside the bandages as Kay begged for answers. "Where am I? Was I in an accident?" She clung to his hand. Despite all the earlier tension, at least she had him by her side. His touch reassured her.

But an icy chill entered his voice when he spoke again. "I didn't want it to be this way, but I had no recourse. You wanted to leave me, and I couldn't let that happen. I've been talking with the other mates from Made to Order about my dilemma and how to proceed. We even met once down at the bookstore. You women can never see how you hurt the men in your lives. You refused to see what you were doing to me, so I removed your eyes. Some of the discarded mates gave me the instruments and tranquilising agents for just such an emergency. I prayed I would never need to use them."

Helpless, Kay grasped the blankets with shaky hands and whimpered.

"Mr Tyler warned me about the fickleness of women, but I didn't want to believe him," he said, his voice hurt and betrayed. "Too often you women cast aside your new mates, like a pile of old rubble, with no regard for our feelings. Most women can't accept true love. Without your eyes, you can't leave. You will be totally dependent upon me and my love. I'll remain your dearly devoted partner forever, for eternity, and like it or not, you will always be my number one priority."

KELLY PINER is a practicing Clinical Psychologist. Her short story "Lazy River" was accepted for publication in Weirdbook's upcoming zombie issue. "Halloween Pie" recently won the Halloween contest sponsored by Spookbrain, and her dark Christmas story "O Christmas Tree" was just selected for the Dark Lane Christmas Anthology. *Her short story "Baggage Claim" was published on Page 47 at be-a-better-writer.com. She has also published stories in* Drunken Pen Writing *and* The Literary Hatchet. *She just completed her first novel,* FAT SANDS.

SUPERSTITIOUS
Lindz McLeod

Despite Kennedy's best efforts, the mirror had broken the baby.

Cassie lay on the floor in six uneven pieces. Part of a torso, attached to a leg. Half a hand. An upper arm and a slice of pudgy ribcage. Her head was mostly intact; red mouth wide open, bawling out a throatful of sweet country pain. She wasn't gonna be no singer, that was for sure.

"Why you do that, baby girl?" Kennedy bent, shuffled the pieces back together as best she could. Her fingers dipped through the edges. She had to focus hard to grip them, so hard her vision swam. Lord, but she was starving. "I can't pick you up 'less you solid, you know that."

The noise increased. Kennedy shook her head. She couldn't hear herself think with all that squalling going on.

"Naw, girl. What we learned 'bout mirrors? Huh?"

The baby's mouth closed part-way but her bottom lip stayed stuck out. The noise lessened to a high-pitched whine.

"You learned nothin'? Huh?"

Eli stuck his head through the wall. "What'd she do now?"

Kennedy straightened up. Eli pressed his hand against the air between them, like they was making a slow motion high five; his wispy body drifted towards her, a full foot off the ground.

"She got at the mirror again. I jest can't keep her away from it." She replicated his movement, palms held inches apart. She missed touching him. Regular stuff; kissing him before breakfast, his arm around her while they watched a movie. He pretended not to notice, sniffing hard as if he'd been running. Pulled his hand back, wiped his nose on the back of his wrist.

"When you gonna learn, kid?" He crouched down, leaning over the shards that made up their daughter. She could see the doorframe right through his grey chest. The shattered pieces were fusing together again, like watching a banana peel filmed backwards.

"Maybe she won't learn. She can't grow none 'til we eat, so maybe she can't remember. I keep telling her to stay away from that dang mirror, but she won't listen."

"Listen, they movin' soon. I heard the agent on the phone, said they was gonna move in. This week, or maybe next."

"They said that last week. And the week before that."

"Baby, I'm sorry.' The muscle in his jaw jumped. 'Can't do nothin' 'bout the livin', you know that."

"I been so hungry, Eli. I don't know how much more I can take."

Cassie came back together with a sound like a zip being drawn up. Not yet old enough to walk, but a damn good crawler. On the day they'd died, she'd had on a pretty red dress over a white blouse; she was stuck in that cute little outfit every day now. Her skin was a creamy pink, bulging the way babies did when they was young and fat; her flesh way more substantial than Kennedy's. She'd given their child everything she had. Every atom. Was it gonna be enough?

Eli stood up. He stepped closer to her, like he wanted to put his arms around her. But he couldn't touch her, didn't even try. They was too faded.

"I know, darlin'. We gonna eat real soon."

The family moved in; momma was a doctor, daddy was some kinda lawyer for poor people. One grandma and one unmarried aunt, plus three kids—two older boys and a young girl—made seven. A good-sized family unit, and kids was always good for eating. The boys didn't tease their sister much, which Kennedy thought was funny, 'cause she was a good few years younger. They treated her like she was real expensive, like she could break any minute.

She'd been sick, apparently, sick for a long time. Something in her brain, maybe a swelling or something. It made the kid quiet. Not slow. Just quiet. She didn't say much. Ate her dinner up, did what she was told. Not restless like her brothers, or like the friends they brought home, who were always moving and laughing, whip-fast. She didn't backtalk none neither. Kennedy wondered if Cassie would be like that, if her daughter would ever grow up. Time moved funny for haunters. It slowed down when the house was empty, sped up when they had a family to eat off. They hadn't had a family in the house for a long time; how much time, she couldn't guess, but the cars outside looked real different and nobody wore hats no more.

She had forgotten how much the first night with a new family hurt; like getting just one bean at a time when you coulda eaten your dog and probably everybody's else's dog too. But they pushed through it. It wasn't as if they had any choice. The next stage was where it started gettin' good, but the pain came first. It always came first. It reminded her of being alive, without the good stuff.

"Who you wanna eat?"

She liked the way Eli let her take the lead. Things had been different, back when they was alive. Men didn't listen to women so much then. She liked to think she'd proved how smart she was, and how smart it made him to appreciate that about her.

"I don't know." Kennedy chewed her thumb. "We need to make sure they stay here longer than the last folks."

Cassie was crawling around their ankles, gurgling and tugging at the straps of her own dress. The study was full of boxes. They stood inside the wall, looking into the room; 'cause they was dead, they was thin, skinny like splinters. The walls was as big as closets to haunters. Space to hide, space to breathe.

"Maybe the daddy? He's still in the kitchen, reading a letter. Looked like he was gonna cry."

Eli's mouth crooked up on one side, the way he used to do when he picked her up for dates. She fell in love with that mismatched smile. He'd told her boys used to make fun of him, joke that he looked like a caught fish with a hooked lip. That wasn't true. The other side curved up afterwards, like a little brother whose legs haven't grown enough yet to keep up with the big boys.

"Whatever you say, boss."

She swatted at him, her hand stopping just shy of his shoulder. "You wanna start?"

"Naw girl, you go right ahead."

She hesitated.

"You said you was hungry. Ain't you?" He squinted at her, seemed to really take in how transparent she was. "Kennedy, how long you been like this?"

"I don't know."

"Can you see the light?"

She didn't want to lie to him, not outright. "A little. Out the corners of my eyes. Not full on."

He sucked air through his teeth. His hands clenched, held stiffly by his sides. "Why the hell didn't you say nothin'?"

She shrugged. It wouldn't have done no good. She didn't want to worry him into his second grave.

"I'm okay. I can't start it but I can join in."

Eli floated forwards, following the wall along and to the left, where it joined the hallway. Kennedy motioned for Cassie to follow her; the baby scooted along on hands and knees. He kept going until they reached the kitchen. The daddy was still there, one hand propping his head up. A letter lay on the table in front of him. Eli squared his shoulders and raised his hand, concentrating. The letter trembled. The daddy looked around at the window, looking for a breeze. The window was shut. He frowned, rubbed his eyes, resumed his position.

The momma came in, all big hair and big smiles. "How're you doing, sweetheart?"

The daddy broke off reading, rubbed his eyes. "Not great. I can't spare the time for this case—not with the Samuels trial coming up—but this letter breaks my heart. I didn't start this practice to turn people away when they need me."

"You can't help everyone."

"Is that your professional opinion?" The daddy had meant this as a joke, but Eli twisted his hand up mid-sentence; the daddy's voice came out rougher than intended. A note of seeded bitterness.

The momma turned away, put the kettle on without replying. The hurt came off her in a thin, purple smoke-ring. Eli gestured again, his face strained from the effort. The smoke-ring drifted towards the wall. He opened his mouth, bit it right out of the air. He clutched his chest. "Goddammit, that hurts. Let me do one for you. Sooner we get this over with, the better."

The momma and the daddy couldn't hear him. Live people closed their ears off to haunters, unless they was asleep or scared. Then they picked up on every floorboard squeak, every soft rustle, every muttered word.

"I didn't mean it like... oh, hell, Vee." The daddy stood up.

Eli crooked his fingers. "She's gonna remember a time when she lost three patients in a row." He listened to the silence between unsaid words. "She was so tired. And he was too busy trying to save some thief-turned-killer from the electric chair, that he forgot to pick the kids up from school."

The daddy tried to put his arms around the momma, but Eli flicked upwards and the momma pushed him off. Another purple smoke-ring erupted from the top of her head and drifted towards the wall, while a square of bright green hurt puffed from the daddy's chest. Kennedy stretched, caught the purple smoke-ring. It tasted like tar but went down like a steak dinner. Pain lashed across her chest. She bent double, too late to catch the green square; it faded away into nothing. She held up her hand to Eli, to signal she was okay, to keep going. Her breath slid into her lungs, like a tin cup dragged across bars. A jud-jud-jud draw of air. Eli flicked again. The momma took a couple of steps further away.

"Oh dang. The way all the other mommas looked at her, when it came out that he was defending a white boy who killed two black men. All they whispers in the schoolyard. That didn't feel so good, huh?" Eli's breaths came in harsh bursts, yanked out from his chest. "I can't hardly believe this guy myself. What's he doing fighting for white folks when he black as night?" He leaned forward against some invisible force; his hair streamed as if he was caught in a wind tunnel.

"Maybe he don't care none about colour."

"Everybody care about colour."

She refused to be drawn into this again. "Eli, don't push too hard. It's been a long time."

"I won't. They busting open." He turned his shoulder and set it against the force. The momma and daddy were looking at each other like they was about to box. "Ripe as you like. Barely needs any—"

Cassie screamed in the distance.

"Baby!" Kennedy hurtled through the wall, back to where her daughter lay in smashed pieces yet again. "Oh honey darling, why can't you stay away fro—"

The quiet girl was looking into the mirror. Her brown eyes were wide, afraid but not terrified. Her hair stuck out from her head, forming a perfect sphere. It jiggled as she tilted her head. She was short for her age, had to stand on tip-toes to see her reflection. Her fingers pressed the glass. Pieces of Cassie lay only inches away, squalling her hurt for the world to hear. The little girl drew a heart shape on the glass, tapped the middle of the shape over and over.

"Jesus Christ. You stay away from my daughter." Kennedy stepped up to the window. "Don't you come tempting her when she don't know no better."

The little girl looked past Kennedy to where the smashed pieces lay.

"Hey. You hear me?"

The kid ignored her. She breathed on the glass and wrote a name on the mist, but it was too hard to read. The kid shook her head and breathed again, exaggerating the breath, and drew the name backwards so Kennedy could read it. JENNY.

"Get gone."

The kid couldn't hear her; she didn't smile, she didn't scowl. Just kept on looking into the mirror.

The momma appeared. "Baby girl, come here and let me do your hair."

The girl allowed herself to be positioned, patiently adjusting to accommodate the momma, but her eyes never left the mirror. The momma held a hairband between her teeth, scraped the kid's hair back and started twisting it into bigger strands to tie back. Kennedy watched them, woman and child, both concentrating real hard. They wore the same expression.

Cassie zipped herself back together in the time it took to do the hair. She was quiet as Kennedy had ever seen her, chubby hands reaching for her own curly locks, trying to recreate the action. The girl smiled at the mirror. It didn't warm Kennedy's heart. It scared the shit out of her.

The family was full of good eatin'. In a few weeks, Kennedy couldn't see the light no more, not even out of the corners of her eyes. Eli looked more solid, his skin several shades closer to the brick-baked colour he had while they was alive. The only problem was that Kennedy couldn't understand why Cassie was getting greyer. They had a good supply now. She should be getting stronger, but she wasn't. And Kennedy couldn't keep her away from that goddamn mirror.

"I think she keeps trying to go through. To get to that little girl."

Eli lay down on the floor and let Cassie crawl through his body. He stayed still, only peeking at her every now and then, so she'd giggle and try to beat his chest with her tiny fists.

"How come?"

"I don't know. She ain't seen no kids in a while. Maybe she's lonely."

"Do you think she can?"

She shrugged. "How am I supposed to know? We came into this together. Nobody gave me an instruction manual."

Eli lifted his hand, folded them into a plane shape. They soared through the air, accompanied by the brumming of his lips. The baby shrieked in delight.

"Maybe one of us should do it. See if there's a weak spot."

Kennedy stared at him. "You know it hurts like hell to get mirror-broke. We both done it before. It don't work."

"Maybe she can see something we can't."

"Like what? She's two years old. What can she see?"

"Well, what else are we supposed to do?"

"I don't know."

"Stop saying that."

"Well, I don't. Asking me ain't gonna produce a new answer." A flash of movement in the doorway of the bedroom made Kennedy whirl. "Look, here she is. Jest watch."

The kid approached the mirror, breathed on it, wrote the word "hello". Eli sucked air through his teeth. The kid waited. Cassie started to wriggle forwards, towards the mirror.

"No, baby." Kennedy caught her around the waist, held her firm.

Cassie began to cry, a howling lament. She reached for the kid, little fingers grabbing for the mirror. The kid raised both hands to the mirror and pushed, her palms paling with the effort, her big brown eyes filling with tears.

*

Kennedy spent a lot of time watching the family. They was kind of entertaining, once you got to know each of 'em and their little ways.

One night, the momma and daddy was in their bedroom. Momma had been reading a book, daddy had been brushing his teeth. Kennedy could smell the mint all the way across the room. It was a different kind of mint than the one she knew, a colder, greener smell. The momma had laid the book down on her lap, one finger keeping her place.

"I don't know if I like it here."

"What do you mean?" The daddy had a mouthful of toothbrush, but his words were understandable.

"This house. It gives me the creeps. Nessie keeps talking about how there's cold spots everywhere."

"I knew whatever house we picked, she was going to find something wrong with it. You know, she doesn't have to live with us." The sound of spitting, a tap running.

"Ma needs the help."

"They could live nearby. Just not in the same damn house."

"I don't think that's what she meant, anyway. She said she felt like someone was watching her."

"She always thinks someone's watching her. Nobody's ever watching her." The sound of a lid being unscrewed, a gargling noise. More spitting.

"She says she got chills."

The daddy reappeared in the doorway, wearing boxers and an unbuttoned collared shirt. He rolled his eyes.

"Vee, we just moved in."

"I know."

"It's a shorter commute for you, It's a good area for the kids. They school has a great athletics programme. It's ranked second in the entire district for grade results."

The momma didn't say nothin'.

"I did my research." The daddy took his shirt off, balled it up, threw it into the laundry basket. A neat shot. "I know how it is here."

He pulled out a drawer, chose a t-shirt, shrugged it on. Kennedy sniffed. Mint again, the regular kind. Soapy, purple flowers. She would have liked to have put her whole face in that drawer and breathed it right up.

"So, what's this really about?"

"It's really about the house, Robert. It's weird." The momma still hadn't taken her finger out of the book.

"It was a good deal."

"Jenny said she saw something too. When I read her a story last night, she—"

"I'm glad she still has an imagination." The daddy sat down on the bed, his back to the momma. Picked at a loose thread on the bedcover.

"What's that supposed to mean?"

"Nothing. It means what I said."

"I know she's not the same, but you can't avoid her forever. She's still your daughter."

"How dare you!" He turned, fixing her over his shoulder. "I'm here every day, while yo—"

"Oh, you drive her to school, sure. Fix her a sandwich when she's hungry. You sat by the hospital bed, same as I did. But you don't look at her the same. You don't treat her the same."

A muscle in the daddy's jaw jumped once, twice. "She's not the same."

"You mean she's not like you anymore."

He flexed his hands, made them into a church shape.

"We used to do all her English homework together. She used to be able to mould language, make it dance. Reminded me of myself at that age. I thought maybe she'd... if she kept going like that, blossoming, that maybe she'd be able to get the same scholarship I got."

"We can still afford to put her throu—"

"It's not about the money. TJ has his football scholarship, and Junior doesn't want to go to college, anyway. He's got some leaflets about trade work. Maybe carpentry. Says he likes the wood smell, the way a table looks when it's done. Gleaming." He broke off, frowning. "That's not it. Even if they all wanted to go, we'd make it work."

Eli appeared, drifting through the wall, munching on an orange line. When he saw the momma, he raised his hands instinctively and started to push.

"Eli!" Kennedy whispered, although she didn't need to. Live habits died hard. "Knock it off. They talkin' 'bout somethin' important."

Eli waggled his eyebrows at her and kept going, although he slowed the crook of his fingers. She shook her head, mouthed "stop". He ignored her.

The momma stretched out her hand, rested it on top of his. The daddy still didn't look at her. He was staring at the wall. "It's not that. It's that she doesn't talk any more. She doesn't write any more. I used to understand her. I used to know what was going on in her head. Now I have no idea."

The momma sighed. "That's kids, baby."

The daddy pulled his hands away. "No, it's not. You don't understand."

"You're worried that you don't know what our kid is thinking?" The momma threw up her hands. "I barely even know where they are half the time. I don't know what any of our kids are thinking."

The daddy stood. "No, Vee. I'm worried she's not thinking anything."

He strode out of the room, slamming the door behind him. The momma sat back on the bed, pulling her legs up to her chest and wrapping her arms around them. She wasn't crying, but her eyes looked red all the same.

A purple smoke-ring wafted out of her hair and towards Eli, who ate it. He licked his lips. Kennedy turned away.

"Ain't you hungry?"

She was, but the scene had turned her stomach. "Naw." Cassie crawled around her feet. "Come on, baby girl."

"I could get something real good out of her now. Baby, wait." Eli was already raising his hands, watching the momma closely. "I'll get you something good."

"Don't bother." She drifted back through the wall.

The little girl had started to inspect each mirror, before and after school. Her brothers hadn't noticed, too busy jostling their friends on the way to play basketball in the yard. The daddy had asked the kid what she was doing. She'd shrugged. He'd turned away but turned back just as quickly. The momma's words were still ringing around in his soul.

"What're you looking for, Jenny?"

"Nothing."

"You sure?"

He'd waited. Silence. He held in a sigh and went into the kitchen. The kid waited 'til she heard the sound of the fridge opening before she got up close with the mirror.

"Come and play, little girl." Her breath fogged up the glass. "I won't hurt you. We won't be lonely if we're together."

Kennedy ate, but she didn't have much of an appetite these days. The baby was greyer than ever; the cream and olive pattern of the wallpaper showing clear through her skin.

"We need to do it together," Eli said. "I can't get as much on my own, you know that. Get a big bite for Cassie. She'll be fine after she eats."

"They gonna burn out. You already usin' 'em up too fast. Momma and daddy fighting again this morning and this time they didn't stop when the kids came in. We need to be careful, Eli."

"I'm careful."

"More careful than that."

The pattern was repeating itself. She could see it play out, stretching off into the distance. Eli had drunk the last two families dry within six months. He'd always been like that—react first, think later. But they had to put the baby first. They tried everything—tried to chop the smoke into little bits for her with their fingers, tried to send it directly into her mouth. Cassie turned away, mouth pursed, squirming to get down, get on the floor, get back to the mirror. Kennedy held her baby tight, pacing up and down, wishing the good feelings could leak through her skin into Cassie's. Nothing worked. It seemed like since her daughter seen that kid, everything she wanted was on the other side of the mirror.

"What's so good about that kid, huh? Why you want her so bad? Why don't you want to stay with us?" She was squeezing Cassie too much, the baby mewling in complaint. "Why ain't I enough for you?"

The baby's little fingers explored the shape of Kennedy's lips, her cheeks wetted with tears. Cassie put her fingers in her own mouth, sucked the salted water from them.

"Mmm." It was almost a *Ma* but not quite.

"Again? You can do it. Say Ma, Cassie. Say Mama."

"Me." Cassie pointed to herself. "Me."

Kennedy heard her own heart cracking. It sounded like getting mirror-broke.

The sun poured puddles of light onto the carpet in the living room. Eli had been pushing the family all night, and a fight had broken out over lunch. The little girl lay on her stomach, colouring in a picture. She used the right crayons and went slow, staying inside the lines. The daddy sat in a chair nearby, nursing a glass, his eyelids drooping in the heat of the room.

"I got a feeling. I think it's gonna be today." Kennedy put Cassie down, and turned to face Eli. "We can't keep putting it off. We can't keep her here. Not if she's got a chance. If she could be on the other side, maybe she cou—"

"How?" His big fists clenched. "She's dead, Kennedy. We dead. You got that? We don't come back, jest from wishing. We done. This is it—this is all we got now."

"Maybe she ain't done! You don't know."

"I do know." He shifted from one foot to another, lips crushed against each other like angry lovers.

"Well, I think you're wrong. I think we got too used to being haunters, Eli. We remember how things used to be and we don't want to forget that and we can't move on. Cassie don't know none of that. Maybe she can have something more."

"What? No! We can't jest—"

"Yes, we can."

Eli spun, red-faced, loomed over her. "She's our *baby*. Don't you care?"

"I care enough to let her go. She gots to go, and she gots to go now."

"What kind of life is she gonna have? Living with these people? Living inside a little girl's head, no body of her own?" Tears drove down his cheeks in two parallel lines; he made no move to wipe them away. "She'd be some kinda parasite! You think that's okay? Our kid, reduced to a goddamn whisper in some black kid's head?"

She'd thought of that already, been thinking about it for days. Cassie had made her choice. Her little body was so young, but she'd been haunting as long as they had, and something about this kid was drawing her out. Kennedy couldn't deny that the kid saw how much Cassie needed out. She was doing them a favour, rather than the other way around.

"Go on, girl. Say goodbye to your daddy." She stooped and kissed the baby over and over on her soft head.

He ignored this. "What about me an' you?"

"We need to Fade. We hung on long enough." She felt, rather than heard, the bone-quivering rumble of a distant train—the kind of train that didn't run on no tracks, but whenever wherever it was drove— and over it, the faint strain of a solo fiddle, high as a scream, high as a star. "Hear that? The red man's comin'. And when he gets here, I wanna be ready for the Judgement. I wanna meet him on my feet."

"K, I can't! I can't do it." He pressed his knuckles to his lips. "I'm scared."

"I guess they families was scared too, huh? When Robert left that package on their doorstep? When John burned a cross into their lawn? When your friends strung 'em up after they didn't leave? Was they scared then, Eli? Did it ever make you stop? Did you ever say it wasn't right?"

His body shook, sobs following one after the other like earthquakes. "It wasn't my hands on the gun. Wasn't my rope neither."

She regretted not being able to slap him. "You think it matter whose rope it was? We did nothing. That's bad enough. Ain't you learned nothing? The world changed while we weren't in it. We gotta take every stripe from now on. And don't be expecting salvation handed to you 'cause I don't think we getting any. We been stuck in this place for a long time so don't you dare tell me you didn't learn nothin'."

"We been nice to these people! Don't that count? Don't that count for somethin'? We died leaving one of them packages, ain't that punishment enough? I'm sorry we did it, okay? I'm sorry! I thought we were different. I thought we were better."

She shook her head, thinking of the living lies she'd told, the webs she'd spun to save people she knew. People like her; like they was the only people who mattered. They was her words, coming out of her mouth. Her choice to speak them. Such a long time ago, but the past was a long scar in the making. If you picked at it enough, it'd bleed same as a fresh one.

"I can't leave Cassie—"

"She didn't do nothin' wrong, Eli! If you truly love her, leave her be."

The sound of the fiddle multiplied like rabbits until it filled every thought in her head and she was busting up with the need to fly, to run wild until her heart burst, to fling herself on the mercy of the merciless.

Cassie was crawling towards the mirror again. The little girl was standing on the other side, colouring abandoned, hands outstretched to receive a baptism of spirits. Kennedy closed her eyes. When she had been rounded with life in her belly, everybody rushed to tell her that letting your baby bird fly free was the hardest thing; that watching 'em grow up and leave the nest would be heart-breaking. She knew now that wasn't true. The hardest thing was letting go of yourself, that selfish part of you that wanted to control the world, make it comfortable and convenient for you and you alone.

Devil take her. She was ready to go.

LINDZ McLEOD is a queer, working-class writer from Scotland, whose short stories have been published by or are forthcoming in the Scotsman *newspaper,* Twist in Time, Cossmass, Wrongdoing Magazine, The New Guard, *and more. She is represented by Headwater Literary Management.*

FADE INTO YOU

Meg Sipos

"What would I have left if I gave you everything?" Amara ran her hand over the tousled sheet, smoothing out the creases, before looking at the man whose chest her head had been resting on. She had picked him up at the bar two nights ago because she hated being alone.

This question had become a tradition of hers, often asked after sex. A challenge of sorts, really. Usually the men in her bed answered with grand promises, their eyes wide with want.

This man studied her, face melting into an expression one might use to admonish a child, the answer obvious on his tongue before the word even tumbled out.

"Nothing."

The weight of his voice spurred something deep in Amara's gut that she didn't quite understand. A weird, foreign feeling that itched and nagged and thrilled.

Still, she schooled her face. Kept her smirk in check and relaxed her slightly crinkled eyebrows. Tried to remain completely impassive as his fingers ran through her tangled hair and tugged at the wild knots.

She took a moment to drink in his hooded eyes and sharp cheeks and pointed chin. Conventionally gorgeous, she thought. Which was always its own pleasure. But that certainly wasn't why she'd chosen him.

"What would you give me if I gave you everything?"

He was the ninth man she had picked up at the bar in the last three months.

It had started as a bothersome itch. A dulled need. She often ventured into the night and sought out the lone men hunched over their half-full beers and empty shot glasses. The ones too absorbed in their own troubles to seek out companionship, but always open to the opportunity to leave their lives behind for a night.

She lured them back to her home with promises of that brief kind of intimacy. The kind that lifted you out of isolation for a moment of euphoric oneness and let you retreat back into yourself, unscathed, after. She told herself she'd never been interested in anything more.

She'd seen more shatter lives.

"Nothing," he told her, his left arm curling her into his chest while his forefinger just barely stroked her nose.

But she could never help herself when she coaxed her nameless men into lingering the next morning with bacon and eggs and toast. Or when she spooned her special sugar into their coffee while she offered them a chance at a possible future together.

She liked watching them entertain the idea, eyes fogging with the allure of something new; something full of untapped potential and possibility. They never entertained the idea of staying with her for very long, though. Once they finished their breakfast, they would sheepishly admit they had a family to return to. Maybe a wife. Sometimes a boyfriend. Always a partner.

She enjoyed nodding in understanding as they stumbled out the door, already a little unsteady on their feet. The knowledge that they had, indeed, given her their future satisfied her enough. There was a certain kind of comfort in knowing they never actually made it home.

They had made such grand promises, after all.

This man in her bed—he was different from the rest. He made no promises, but he had stayed. For two nights.

She thought he might when she had approached him, hunched over his fifth shot of whiskey and cradling his seventh beer, eyes still startlingly lucid when they combed her over. She found the spark of anger and now-whining ache inside her thrilling at the sight. That was why she had chosen him.

"And what do you want from me?" she asked, her hand resting on his chest, the warmth of his skin against hers offering only prickling emptiness.

She wanted to feel more than that—more than the constant gnawing inside.

"Everything."

So Amara gifted him her name and her hands, loose and soft on his skin. She gifted him her trust. Gave him all of herself. Still, she received nothing in return.

For six months, the man stayed while Amara emptied herself out for him. She leaned into his gentle, ghost-like caresses and still he gave her nothing. She nipped at his neck while he gripped her hips with his nails and gave her nothing.

The once only bothersome itch began to nag at her every odd hour of every odd day. Sometimes, at night, she wrapped her legs around his hips and willed him to swallow her whole—to absorb her into his own skin.

Still, he gave her nothing.

So she began leaving him little love notes written in her own blood. The shape of a heart on the mirror and the fridge. X's and O's on the bedroom window and the door.

She chopped off the smallest toe on her left foot. Dressed the newly severed piece of herself in a bow and left it nestled on the pillow the man used, like a neatly wrapped chocolate on a hotel bed. She grated flakes of her skin over the meals she cooked and mixed her hair into the coffee grounds before brewing. And she never even put her special sugar in his coffee.

Amara waited for *thank yous* and *I love yous* that never came. The man never once spoke of her romantic gestures.

"What do I have left to give?" She asked one night while his hands grazed her arms, his face half-hooded by the shadow of his pillow.

Breathless, she waited for him to say nothing. She waited for him to give her something *more* than nothing. Instead, he offered an empty smile, as though disappointed.

"Everything."

When the everything she could offer wasn't enough—when *she* wasn't enough—the man who had only ever given her nothing left.

For several weeks, Amara waited for the numbness of his loss to wash over her. Instead, the ache inside her twisted and bubbled and seared. On the third week, the growing itch became an insatiable need to scratch her way out of her own skin.

Huddled between the sink and toilet on the bathroom floor, Amara scraped her fingernails against her raw, reddening flesh until it began to peel away and reveal muscle. She found herself gazing down at the skin she had shed, her arms oozing puss and blood, dissatisfied.

It wasn't enough.

The itch still lingered.

So she continued to peel away at her flesh.

She couldn't bring herself to stop.

She wondered, briefly, if she might claw her way into the void.

Eventually, after an entire night collapsed on her bathroom floor itching, itching, *itching*, the ache dulled. The incessant, unforgiving need driving her to chip away at herself finally relaxed into that numbness she had been waiting for.

After, when she came back to herself, she felt calm and detached, but also uncomfortably naked in a way she'd never known before. Exposed.

The itch alleviated at least for the moment, she stumbled to her feet.

Stiffly, she ventured into her yard and began gathering fallen cherry blossoms with numb fingers. She and the man who had given her nothing, the man who had left—breathing—*alive*—had watched them bloom from the bedroom window. He had smiled when they wilted and drifted to the ground.

Looked satisfied at the brevity of their beauty.

Now, Amara peeled the fallen blossoms off the grass and studied their pink-hued petals before sticking them to blistering muscles, to what was left of her skin, in an effort to hide the only pieces of herself she had left.

MEG SIPOS holds a BFA and MFA in creative writing. Her work has appeared or is forthcoming in Moon Park Review, Lammergeier Magazine, The Ghost Story, Quantum Shorts, Bath Flash Fiction, Liminality, *and* 21st Century Ghost Stories: Vol. II.

SWEETROOTS

Ashley Van Elswyk

I wake a few feet below the surface, half-tangled in hyacinth roots. The earth presses down on me, cool and slightly damp, and the roots tickle where my hands fold awkwardly over my chest.

In this heavy darkness, I can't stretch out, let alone blink.

There isn't much left of myself, that's obvious, but strangely, the absence of flesh doesn't affect my ability to feel. Stones and sweet-smelling dirt mould around my skeletal body, push through an open jaw to fill the gaps in my face. One larger rock digs between the vertebrae of my spine, and if I still had a throat to block I'd certainly be choking. I'm not even sure if I'm breathing.

I must be dead, right? Buried without coffin or shroud, and for a long while, clearly, given my bone-deep nakedness. But how could I be dead when I'm awake to consider this cramped grave enveloping me? A corpse shouldn't know she's a corpse.

"... grown more quickly than I..."

A woman's voice, silvery and distant. Despite the earth between us, it sounds as if she's right beside me, and I instantly latch onto the sound.

If she speaks, I won't feel so lonely.

Please speak again.

"You—you're awake! Oh, wonderful!" the voice exclaims. A faint thud indicates she's knelt down above me. "No need to panic, I'm here to take care of you. I suppose you could call me your gardener."

My gardener? What use has a corpse for a gardener? Certainly a priest, maybe a gravedigger in certain instances—even a resurrectionist, fates forbid, although I doubt there's enough of me left to bother unearthing. Will she tend the grass around my grave?

I'm reminded suddenly of the too-long hyacinth roots braiding around my fingers and ribs, binding my wrists together at my breast. A nagging suspicion prompts me to shift my attention outward.

And so discover that beyond the soil and stones and hungry little grubs, I've missed all the other roots.

An astounding number, really. Thin little wisps, some still attached to split seed-shells, others thick as ropes winding down from the surface. Pale veins of the earth, spreading deeper, deeper, all around. Knotting around my remains in a strange imitation of the muscle I've lost, holding me in place. I don't need to see the above-ground petals to know what they are. Some clusters come from the same plants, but there's more—pansies, camellias, rhododendron, zinnias of all colours, milkweed, laceflowers, even a lilac sapling, and at the edge of the plot, a scattering of delicate verbena. So, so many more.

My grave is shrouded in a symphony of flowers.

The woman—Gardener—jolts me from my thoughts again. "You should know I can understand you. Only a little, not so much in words as a... *feeling* of sorts." She hums, apparently dissatisfied with her own answer. "Well, it's better than nothing, yes? I expect we'll come to communicate a little clearer in the future. I realise this might be difficult to come to terms with, especially waking up after this long. But now..."

Thrusting her hand into the earth, she digs and twists through softened soil until her nails scrape against my bones. She grips my wrist tightly, and I feel warm flesh, the steady thrum of a pulse guiding blood through her living veins.

Above, she whispers, "Blossom. Thrive. I'll take care of you, my most precious flower. You'll see the sun again, eventually. I promise."

I almost believe her. But then her hand is gone, and the hole fills in, and it's hard to trust that the sun exists at all. It hurts to hope. Hope chews uncomfortably at me like a thorn-toothed worm, so I let it sour into something I can wrestle down and bury.

What good is the sun to me, anyway? Don't the dead belong to this dark, deep under the ground?

Precious flower, this stranger called me. As if I were something more than a simple rotting corpse, guised in gardens.

One day, Gardener mentions my burial. "You wore yellow. Do you remember? Maybe it should have been funny, in an odd way, but for some reason I've always found it sad. Like burying sunshine." She hums, rakes her fingers through the surface soil in patterns around the stems, not quite scratching my itch.

I've no choice but to trust her words. I hadn't been awake then, and there's not much left of myself down here to remember by, let alone any scraps of a yellow dress.

"After the dirt settled, it left such an ugly mound. Empty. I couldn't… Leaving it like that seemed cruel. You were meant for so much better. So I built you a new home filled with colour and life, so I'll always be with you, even when I'm not here."

It's interesting to know she saw me before I was sealed into the grave, the dark. Almost reassuring. She's seen my face, and I envy her, because I haven't seen hers in turn.

"So beautiful. Seemed almost a shame at first, to…" she murmurs, trailing off. Had she not meant for me to hear that last part? I stifle my curiosity before she senses. "And now, here, you are beautiful again."

The stems tremble at her careless brushes, down to my captor roots, mimicking a shudder.

"Oh, if only you could see how your garden has grown! I said I'd take care of you, didn't I?"

I'm not concerned with the garden's progress; she's far more intriguing. Try as I might, I can't stop thinking of the way her nails felt against me, that first day. I wonder if she caught a fragment of me in that touch, carried it back to the surface. Skin or bone dust, washed away in the sun. She hasn't touched my body since. I want her to, and she must realise this, but she only offers me words; keeps her caresses for the flowers.

She tends the gardens holding me down, and then she leaves.

*

"Would you like to hear a story?" Gardener asks.

It's a hot day—the earth bakes under the glare of the sun's rays. Not that I can enjoy such heat down here. The roots feel a little limper than usual, and I tug them curiously, testing. An opportunity. She'll water them before she leaves, but for now, there's time.

I project interest up, then stretch out as best I can. A few silky tendrils slip between the gaps of my spine, sending a pleasant jolt through me.

She pulls a few wayward weeds as she speaks. "A girl neared the end of a long journey. As she made her way across meadows and forest, darkness crept up quicker than she'd expected. Realising she wouldn't make it home before sunset, she stopped to make camp, and unknowingly laid herself to rest upon an unmarked grave."

Between words, she goes about the rhythmic, ritual work of gardening: tending the sprouts, weeding, watering. Her story is accompanied by the crunch of a metal trowel against soil, and the hum of a familiar tune, simple and repetitive, one which always lulls me into thoughtlessness.

"The girl eventually arrived home, and soon after discovered that she'd become the carrier of an unsettled ghost. Indoors and outdoors, it lingered, always in the corner of her eyes, at her back, its cold hands slipping tighter around her neck. Haunting her night and day.

"Eventually, she fled from her home to wander the world, trying to find the grave. To return the spirit to rest."

Gardener's voice settles into empty silence instead of the end of her story. I squirm against the roots, dissatisfied. The dirt shifts, the bindings loosen.

Is that all? The story ended so abruptly. Did the girl succeed? It's nice to believe that after all those sleepless nights of digging, the girl at last uncovered the age-stained bones of her ghost, and both were finally able to rest peacefully.

But then they'd each be alone again. At least when the girl was haunted, she wasn't alone. And what of the poor ghost? Forced back down to a forgotten grave, nameless, unwanted and abandoned? I can't help but sympathise.

It's lonely and cold under the ground.

Indecision, and a queer sliver of envy, leaves me unsure of my own desire, whether I hope she succeeded, or…

"If you'd like to imagine a happy ending, go ahead. I can't say for certain whether she found it. Personally, I prefer a different version— I've heard one where the poor girl goes mad roaming the moors, cursed to spend forever digging with a ghost at her heels; in another, the ghost waits until she's at her weakest, then steals her body. But I suppose I always have been… enthralled, by tragedy," Gardener muses.

Tragedy? The intimacy of becoming one with another... is strangely far from disturbing. I let the idea settle in my mind for a moment before quickly discarding it. I think I'd much prefer to remain beside my gardener than become her.

"With this garden covering your burial site, you shouldn't be disturbed, and tempted to haunt someone else. I hope you'll never feel the need to leave the ground. But if you did, I don't think I'd mind if you chose to follow me," she says, almost wistfully. "I don't think I'd mind at all."

I believe her.

But what will happen when winter comes? I wonder at her. *When the world is buried in snow, and the flowers are as dead as I?*

Gardener leans down. "I will keep your garden alive, by any means. Build a new one, to hold you until spring returns," she says, her breath seeping through the ground to press against my cheek. Carrying the sweet honey of her lips. "I will keep you alive."

Lay across my grave then, and become the garden yourself. Nothing less will satisfy, I silently demand. *You've ruined the rest of the world for me.*

Because I don't want flowers. I don't need sunlight, or stories. I want her to lay down so I may pull her under, into a sunless bed, death's embrace. She can join me within the earth. That's the only way I'll ever feel warm again—when her soft flesh covers my aching bones.

I'm so hungry. Wanting.

Dirt slides across my bones, shifting as I chisel away at my tomb with tiny nudges and jerks. Gradually breaking around me. I'm gleefully patient with my work—the dead have all the time in the world. And neither I, nor my sweet gardener, have anywhere else to go.

Best of all, as a result of my constant movement, the roots binding me have loosened significantly. An unexpected delight. I yank at them, testing their strength, and every day I find them a little slacker.

Pebbles clack gleefully together around my jaw, harder than laughter.

I've wriggled my way up to the skin of the surface. Made a tiny peephole in the dirt, just enough to let in the sky light—it's dark, but there's one star directly above, filling the hollow of my eye.

The air is near enough to taste. Cool and numbingly heady.

A *need* rushes through me, viciously fearsome. A need to get out, to rip the roots off my bones, to bury the flowers in the ground they imprisoned me under, to soak in every second of sunrise waiting for my gardener to return. Revel in the shock of such unnatural rising.

I must see her. Feel her touch again. But touch isn't enough—there's more, keeping me frustrated and hungry, something I can't grow the words to describe.

I've found more seeds in her absence. They travel through the ground, see, carried by the roots towards me like a magnet drawing metal. There's a little cluster gathered here now, waiting to grow. I pick a few seeds and force them open, push the sprouts towards the sky—*grow, grow*—for her to discover in the morning.

She'll know what it means. Maybe she'll understand what I want, more than I do.

"Well, where did these come from?" Gardener exclaims. She traces the veins of the newly blossomed snapdragon leaves. The roots are twisted around my jaw, and her petting tickles all the way down. "This won't do. Are you trying to tell me something, my flower? Playing games?"

I project innocence, and amusement at the appearance of new growth without her influence. Keeping perfectly still, hiding the rest of the seeds under the base of my skull. Pretending I'm deeper than I am.

But *oh hells* it hurts when she pulls the flowers out. Not physically—those roots aren't strong, they haven't needled their way into the cracks of my bones—but witnessing the deliberate act is as crushing as a blow to the chest.

The temptation to force up another, angrier, seedling is almost irresistible. Miraculously, I restrain myself. Instead, I offer up naïveté, pretending to be saddened at her actions rather than seething.

"It's not your fault, dear flower. Down there, you don't know better," she says, yanking out the last stem. "But I do. If you could see the garden, you'd understand your plant had no place here. It's not beautiful, not worthy of decorating your bed. Please, leave the garden to *me*." Spoken sweetly, with a shadow of warning.

I want to be with you, I plead with as much urgency as I can muster. *Aren't I strong enough to join you?*

"You *are* with me. Always below, where I can keep you safe. Where you will stay."

The earth sours with my mood, and worms wriggle rapidly away from me.

She'll be furious when she discovers what I've done, but at this moment, I don't care.

Roots that once bound me have become the tools of my petty revenge, a new attempt at conveying the nameless desire I'd tried to show her before. That she'd rejected, torn out.

So, I will do the same to her.

One by one, the flowers disappear as I yank the roots, dragging the stems down under earth. The fragile green snaps between my bones. They'll make a lovely bed for me.

Moonlight drips enticingly across the wreckage, barely catching the bones beneath. The ground is littered with peepholes, but rather than enjoying the rare glimpse of open sky, I push the dirt around to fill them in—I don't want to make things easy for her.

Gone at last are the saccharine blooms, ripped apart and drowned. The garden is destroyed and I am satisfied with the work. *My* work, I realise with glee.

As much as I adore my gardener, I revel in this little control I've discovered. I'm tired of being treated like a pet, never trusted; a delicate object, to be decorated but never touched. Tired of being trapped under a garden prison.

I want her to remember that I am no flower.

*

Her fury is exactly as thrilling as I'd imagined.

"What have you done?" Gardener screams, raking her fingers across the bare plot. "You've ruined it, you've ruined everything!"

The ground gives her nothing. I spitefully hold the broken flowers too deep for her to grasp. After a few minutes of her scrabbling, I push one seed to the surface and force it to bloom. A petunia, carrying all of my resentment, my longing for more.

In response, she tears it to pieces.

"After all I've done to build this," she snarls, slamming her palms down over my head. "I only want to be happy. For *us* to be happy. A blissful garden with just the two of us. I've worked so hard for you. If you realised what I sacrificed, what you—" she cuts herself off, and takes a few ragged breaths.

I wait, picking at stray bits of roots, half-frustrated, half-curious.

There's silence, and then she heaves herself onto her feet. A chill creeps into my chest, halting my anger with uncertainty. *Now what?*

"I'm going to replant everything. Rebuild what you've tried to ruin. But I won't speak to you," she says, her voice detached. "In fact, I might never show a single gesture of acknowledgement towards you again. And then how would you live? Think carefully, *my precious flower.*"

The chill rots into an all-consuming terror as I listen to her walk away. Suddenly, the darkness around me is too heavy, a crueller binding than the roots ever were, and I am completely and utterly paralyzed. I feel more like a dead thing than ever.

My gardener plans to abandon me? Soil rattles around my bones, cascading in fragments through my ribs, and I want to scream at the hollowness of myself.

She thinks that because I'm a simple corpse, I cannot have agency? That because she woke me to an unlife I never asked for, she is my keeper, who may dangle her presence like a gift to be snatched away at any time? No. I love my gardener too much to let her leave me like this.

She is mine as much as I am hers. Shouldn't a partnership be made on equal ground, with equal control?

Or, perhaps, made *under* ground.

The idea has been germinating in the pit of my mind for some time, tempting, but never genuinely considered. Before, it hadn't seemed necessary, let alone doable, given she'd had me so intricately bound.

But the image of the two of us, curled up in the same grave... it's irresistible.

Our arrangement could never go on as it had, I reason, poking pale, twig-like fingers through the surface. As long as we remain separated, we'll never truly be happy. If Gardener is too stubborn to take that step, well... she's made enough choices for me already. I have no qualms about making this choice for her. For our love.

Even through my anger, I ache for her. The swell of her voice, lowered in sweetness, in ferocity; the smoothness of her movements, teasing her touch through the roots—and touch, that single warm brush of flesh which has haunted my every lonely second, a phantom I cannot dispel!

To hold her would elate me beyond dreams.

And I hate her for threatening to withhold it all forever.

When I finally break through the surface and emerge into the fiery glow of my first sunset, the sight is beyond anything I'd imagined from Gardener's stories. Orange and pink dominate the sky, edged with a deep rose red, and it seems a crime not to admire its brilliance.

The ghost of a smile spreads over my teeth. With a flick of my wrist, the cache of seeds I've gathered rises to join me, and every pod and sprig splits open. I bring back the petunias alongside spears of gladioli, cascading vines of morning glories wrapped around chrysanthemums and lilies. Poison plants slipping out from under their rich green leaves. All woven between clusters upon clusters of bright, golden tansys. This display of furious desire, a final gift for my gardener.

Dust and root fragments fall from me as I step back to admire the vicious new flora. Such freedom! I understand the deep affection Gardener had for this pretty petal palette; the ability to change the garden as I please is intoxicating. Flowers grow where I wish, perform my song, embody my heart.

I can see why she'd be so reluctant to share, but it's only fair I have my turn. After all, isn't it my plot?

A few tendrils of hair still clinging to my skull sway in the breeze. The air smells sharp, flush with life. There's another scent too: smoke, carried over from across the clearing.

Clearing?

Empty, open land? When Gardener talked of my funeral, I assumed I was in a cemetery of sorts, but there isn't another plot or headstone in sight, no people, no—

Oh.

I suppose in all the times she fed me stories, she's never mentioned *where* I was buried. Or by whom. Always carefully clipped out.

Wobbling stumbles become steady steps as I move across the grass towards the smoke. I have no doubt it's where I'll find her, bring her home.

The warmth of her presence still permeates the cottage in her absence, like a stone touched by sunshine. An apron I've heard fold against the ground when she kneels hangs on the wooden peg by the door; her trowel lies on the plain oak tabletop. A still-smouldering fireplace clearly originated the smoke I'd followed.

Yes. This is where my Gardener lives.

I don't bother to close the door. She'll be back soon enough, and I want this to be settled quickly. Why waste precious time?

Overall, this front room is neat. Except the seed packets thrown down, spilling their contents across the floorboards, and the mess of fallen books and boxes by the fireplace, suggest an upset. I'm not sorry for angering her, but it's amusing to find she's taken her anger out on her surroundings much the same way I have.

One of the small boxes lies open on the table, and curiosity leads me to examine it. A charming thing, decorated with pressed purple bellflowers under a chipping glaze. I realise instinctively that it's important.

The air grows heavy, and I can barely manage to lift my hand enough to gently lay it across the contents of the box. If I weren't already dead, I might have lost my breath.

Inside the box lies a lock of ash-blonde hair, tied with a scrap of yellow ribbon. And I know that it belongs to me.

Delicate, but foreign. I don't feel the slightest connection to this lock, so different from the muddy strands clinging to my skull. The hair rests weightlessly in my palm.

"You—!"

A gasp from behind drags my attention towards a dark silhouette in the doorway, and *oh*.

Even with her features twisted with shock and horror, the softness I've come to know only through her presence is unmistakable. Bare arms dusted with sun and dirt, dark hair pulled back behind a faded kerchief. Her eyes shine too bright, gleaming with a deep fervour even fear cannot disguise when they fall upon me. I imagine if I still had proper eyes, mine would appear much the same when I see her.

Instead, I deliberately project my want towards her, as I had while underground, in place of a blackening gaze. A thrill rushes through me when her breath hitches.

There's no tongue left in my mouth, but instinct leads me to test what I hope is possible.

"It's lovely to see you."

The words drift from between my jaws like a stray breeze, faint and unguided. There's brief delight in the twitch of her lips, swallowed quickly away.

"You shouldn't be here," Gardener says. Her voice is unimpeded, resonating as clearly through my bones as the sweet trill of the wind chimes outside the cottage.

But not with fear—I should have realised. How could she fear me, her dear creation? No, this is distress. This is someone scrabbling to maintain her composure in the face of an abrupt loss of control. I took the liberty of digging myself up, inviting myself into her home, all without her sweet words to guide me.

"Why?" I ask. "Because you thought you'd assured I couldn't leave the ground? Honestly, those roots weren't terribly strong."

A sprig of indignation. It's fascinating, to spot the emotions so clearly on her face and in the shift of her shoulders; easier than picking apart the tones of a distant voice. And terribly delightful to be able to plant these emotions there myself.

"Or maybe," I continue, "deep down, you wanted me to escape? You did say you wouldn't mind."

Gardener snaps. "Escape? You're talking nonsense. I don't know what you mean by accusing me of trapping you when I was keeping you safe. And now look! You're wandering around getting into everything—who knows where you could have ended up, what might have happened!"

Then she rushes forward and snatches the lock from my hands, before stumbling back, putting the table between us. I circle around to stand before the door.

"What is that?" I ask, wondering how truthfully she'll answer, now she must look at me directly. No earth to hide her, to ease the lies.

"A keepsake."

My teeth click together in place of a tongue. "Why do you need a keepsake? I'm here, aren't I? You can visit me anytime. But, it isn't about missing me, is it?"

She's breathing heavily, eyes flickering between me and the door. Such a soft shade of brown, like rain-damp earth. They linger on me more than the door. Isn't that delightful?

"You needed to hold on to a piece of me, didn't you? After you killed me."

Gardener weaves the lock between her fingers. "Why don't we just go back to the garden?" she says, too lightly. "Get you back in bed, where you belong, and we'll talk—"

"No. I want you to tell me."

Irritation twists her face, breaking the nervousness for a brief moment, and it almost makes me laugh. She doesn't fear me nearly as much as she's tricked herself into believing.

Don't hide yourself, Gardener. Not from me. Be as cruel and gentle as you like, but always be honest.

"Tell me," I say, the whistle in my voice cutting through the air between us.

With that, she breaks.

"Yes. But my love brought you back, just as I planned," she cries, clutching the lock of hair to her chest. I want to rip it out of her hands and grind it into the dirt. Why is she holding onto a dead thing, when I'm standing right here? "You'll stay beautiful, and never leave me. I'll never lose you. I'll take care of you, forever. Don't you want that?"

Remnants of roots continue dripping off me, leaving a trail across the floor. "I can never leave, no. But you can."

An intake of breath like the first fall of dirt into a grave. There's dirt under her nails, crescents smearing onto her shirt as she digs them in, violently twisting the fabric. Or is it blood? Dried blood, the same colour as my plot.

It makes no difference.

"How do I know you won't leave me one day?" I step closer. "How can I be sure *you'll* stay forever?"

"What do you mean? I always come, I'm always—I mean—I will, but—"

She's pale as lilies, pale as bone. She'd look pretty in bone. And wouldn't it be perfect, to be a matching pair?

"Don't you want that?" I echo her sweetly. "Don't you want to stay with me too?"

"I do, my precious flower, I do. But let me—"

"It's lonely under the ground, but I wouldn't be lonely with you. The roots can't hold me, they're too loose, too breakable. Roots spread out to other bodies, but you only want me, right? Won't you hold me?"

She hesitates; a few strands of blonde fall from her hands, and with each one elation blooms in me. I don't give her the chance to answer.

My bones encircle her before she can even open her lips.

When Gardener finally spots the overflowing garden, she hisses and clenches my arm hard enough to nearly break.

"This isn't how it was supposed to be… this is all wrong, you were supposed to behave…"

"Nothing's wrong. I created a new garden for us to share."

Even as she tugs against my grip, she never once attempts the simplest and most obvious means of escape by breaking me. Wouldn't it be easy enough? I am, essentially, only bone. A quick twist, a snap, then freedom. But she holds back. Deep down, even in the flowering face of a waiting grave, she still doesn't want to hurt me.

"I understand what you're feeling. Afraid. I was too. But you must accept that I'm doing this because…" I pause, trying to pick out the right words to sooth her. "Our love will never thrive as long as we are separated by life."

In a snap, Gardener switches tactics and returns to begging. "Please, my flower, reconsider! How can I take care of you if we're both dead?"

"I'm not a flower. I'm a corpse. I don't need to be *taken care of.*" Gently, I push the kerchief off her head and lean in close, my mouth not quite touching her ear. "I just don't want to be alone. What I need, my love, is for you to stay with me. Forever. And since I can't join you in life, you must join me in death."

She shivers, but instead of pulling back again, she surprises me by turning to close the space between us, wrathful and loving. It's the most beautiful sensation in the world. The heat of her lips burns into memory and I almost regret that they won't last underground.

"I hate you," she whispers.

"I hate you," I echo, adoringly.

The ground splits open. Gardener collapses against me, nails raking against bone, a single breath escaping her. I drag her down, and cover us both in roots and dirt and darkness.

High above, the garden grows abandoned and lost to nature. Overrun with a blanket of early spring snowdrops. We don't need it anymore.

What use is the sun, either? The earth is always warm now, and teeming with buried things: squirming creatures, the slow stretch of unseen growth, the decay. A lullaby of life and death. Darkness has become an embrace more than a prison, and nothing remains above-ground to intrigue or tempt me.

I hold Gardener tightly in my arms, so close our bodies are tangled into one. Gardener weaves a heliotrope root around my wrist, draws it back to loop around her own, again and again. Binding us. The pale strands slip between her fingertips, newly bared bones.

ASHLEY VAN ELSWYK is a queer Canadian writer of speculative fiction and poetry. When not writing or daydreaming, she finds inspiration on nature walks. Her work appears in Green Ink Poetry, From the Farther Trees, *and the* Hundred Word Horror: Home *anthology. She can be found on twitter @ashvanewrites.*

THE BUTTERFLY COLLECTOR
Paige Johnson

Some people press chrysanthemums into photo-albums to mourn fizzled-out flames. A poor man's formaldehyde, they trap their loves' perfume and depleted petals beneath a flimsy sheet. I grieve with more flair. That's why I've been a butterfly collector since I was a boy.

It's no secret that girls like a gift showcasing some personality. At the age of eight, I fell face-first for a little sugar-pop named Vanessa. She had a voice softer than her curls. We spent countless afternoons on the school's corroding swing-set, chatting about cartoons and kicking up rocks. Once I was bold enough to express my affections, I started by serenading her with my bitten-up kazoo.

She clapped, and I knew I had an in. I can still feel the scrape of mulch against my knee as I kneeled to give a proper proposal. A symbol of extra chumminess, the promise of exclusive playdates. Popping open a scuffed ring box, I revealed a brilliant blue butterfly. "You can have and name her," I said, "but I have to give the box back to Mother. She doesn't know it's missing yet."

Vanessa gaped, brushing a beetle-black curl behind her ear. "It's so pretty! Like the butterflies I saw at Peach Creek with Mommy."

My breath hitched as I inhaled, hoping I could be the one wandering those tall, purple flowers at the park with her. Maybe dare to hold her hand as we crossed the rickety bridge. "Her polka spots match your hairbow," I pointed out, trying to make my pitch seem more thoughtful than salesman-like. "And her wings match your eyes."

Leaning in to examine the fuzzy body and periwinkle ribbing, she asked, "Where did you get her from? She's so special."

The wider her smile grew, the more my chest fluttered. "The mud on my driveway. Two days ago."

"Wait, what?"

"If it wasn't the weekend, I-I'd have gotten her to you sooner, but—"

"Who'd leave that in your driveway?" Squinting, she poked the specimen with dirt-crested fingernails. For the first time, I noticed how chipped and bitten they were.

"Stop!" I pulled the box to my chest, closing it. "She's delicate."

Vanessa's face crinkled, like the butterfly before I rehydrated her with damp paper towels.

"That's not a toy? A prize ring from the roller rink?" Vanessa looked as though she just swallowed a spoonful of cough syrup.

"Huh? No, she's better than some plastic." I opened the box to admire her again. "She's real."

"Real?" Vanessa's eyes inflated. "S-She's dead?" She tapped a wing before I could pull back. Like stained glass, it shattered.

Her disgusted cry rang across the playground, sending a dozen stares my way. Her screams stung more than the cuts on my knees. She labelled me a killer and a creep, solidifying there'd be no cheek-kisses behind a knotted oak. No interlacing of sweaty palms underneath a moth-grey sky or movie dates paid for with backlogged allowance.

My heart was crushed like the caterpillar she stepped on while storming off. After school, I cradled its corpse, pledging to reassemble everything she broke that day.

At twenty-five, I wonder if I've learned my lesson. Though it's been a while since the schoolyard taunts of "Butterfly Boy" pierced my ears, it's been years since a girl's gaze last quickened my pulse.

Biting my lip, I stare at the pages of my pressing book. Exotic corpses cling to each page, dated like a diary with no intent to kill or desecrate—only to preserve. From larvae to pupa, each butterfly represents a stage in my life, coloured by emotion and named after deceased crushes.

Will my new flame, Julia, ever peruse these pages? Lovingly stroke the edges? Help me raise caterpillars off sugar water in a mesh tent? Let me use her tweezers to unfold the antennae? Mother and Vanessa never appreciated my eccentricities, but someone must, right?

A butterfly's head can turn 180-degrees without harm, so why should I have much trouble changing my perspective? Keeping bullies' slights (and Mother's constant refrain of "Ick, put that away!") from pollinating negative thoughts in this head has been my pastime longer than entomology. Besides, Julia never flinched on our date at the Natural History Museum's ladybug exhibit. And didn't I see her peacefully remove a spider from her apartment a week ago?

At my workbench, I scrutinise her Valentine's present. A blood-orange Monarch shipped from a Filipino farm. She came wrapped in wax paper like a delicatessen delight. I suppose her glass box is an upgrade from refrigerated Tupperware. I just hope Julia finds her fate as charming.

Nerves wriggling like a caterpillar, I enter the candlelit café to find Julia sipping wine. As stunning as a swallowtail, she smiles at me. "I sent the waiter off to get you a chardonnay." She giggles, eyeing the bag in my hand. "What'd you get me?"

I set her gift on the table before my shaking can break it. Sliding it out of its tissue cocoon, I present the butterfly. Staged on a piece of bark garnished with silk petals, she protects pearls meant to simulate eggs. "Thought you'd appreciate a big and bright classic. Plus, it compliments the dress you wore on our date to the apple orchard."

"Oh yeah." Her smile slowly twists. "I remember... You *wanted* worms in the apples."

Lifting the art-piece, I tap the back. "It doubles as a music box if you twist the crank."

"Oh... Neat. *Sure beats those opera tickets I mentioned.*" Her frown deepens. "You washed your hands since putting that together, right?"

"Huh? Of course. Speaking of cleanliness, it's amazing the household products you can use to 'resurrect' these beauties. Floor cleaner as a mould inhibitor, acetone to position them before they re-harden."

I congratulate myself for not mentioning how I injected her abdomen with water to look plumper. Pinned her thorax to keep the wings from tearing during manipulation, wiped off the liquified fat dulling her vibrance, and glued her legs back.

Mood moulted, Julia looks away and gulps her wine. "Uh, you should put that thing away. They serve food here. It's kinda disgusting when you think about it, ya know?"

"Right," I sigh. "Of course."

My fascination has me digging in the dirt again. I guess this lonely passion is why I never learned to connect with others. Caught up in the glimmer of pretty things, I am still too weak to ward off their hatchlings of hate, the infestation.

Like Vanessa, Mother, and my book full of bodies, I have another to add to the collection. Another lifeless specimen who'll never speak to me—or anyone—again.

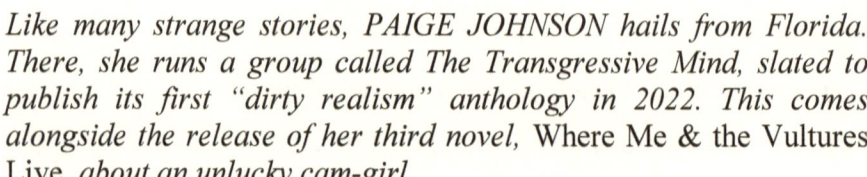

Like many strange stories, PAIGE JOHNSON hails from Florida. There, she runs a group called The Transgressive Mind, slated to publish its first "dirty realism" anthology in 2022. This comes alongside the release of her third novel, Where Me & the Vultures Live, *about an unlucky cam-girl.*

   Fan Page: Facebook.com/ThePoliticiansDaughter

   Fiction Group: Scribophile.com/groups/The-Transgressive-Mind/

BUMPED

Shannon Scott

You get snug in the seat before taking out your phone. As the bus pulls away, you tap in your passcode and watch the screen light up with messages. All for you. Or part of you. The part of you that is *not you*.

A chick sitting in an eggshell reminds you to take your vitamins. A pea in a pod tells you not to eat sushi. A virtual midwife in a medieval wimple assures you that nipple hair is completely normal. Instagram pics appear for new shades in maternity knitwear. Promoted Tweets advertise belly buds to play *Prego with Pavarotti: How to Grow a Prodigy*. If you purchase the belly buds, you get five free morning sickness bags in designs like *sprinkles* and *bamboo*. Now you can look trendy even whilst vomiting in public.

After entering the kick tracker, spotting checker, and pee counter into the app, you're asked if you want the measurements for the week. You're about 20 weeks in, give or take. Your finger hovers between *Parisian Bakery* and *Fruit Bowl*. You make a selection. You are informed that your baby is now the size of an éclair. You can eat it in two bites. But it won't taste like choux pastry and cream.

You close your eyes. It's a summer day. The sun shines in through the bus windows. Fractured by leaves, it creates a kaleidoscope behind your eyelids. You lean back in the seat and expose the bump, not at all surprised when an old man behind you says, "Congratulations."

"Thank you," you say, though you're a little disappointed he doesn't reach out to touch your belly so you can slap his hand away.

"Boy or girl?" he asks.

You shrug.

"Well, if it looks anything like its mama," he says, "it'll be a real cutie pie."

You fold your hands across your bump and rub it protectively, proudly, like a crystal ball. Except it's not a crystal ball. And it's not an éclair either. It's a bicycle helmet, men's size small, wrapped in masking tape and secured to your abdomen with an ace bandage and a pregnancy belt support brace.

20 weeks earlier, give or take.

You retch into the toilet bowl. You're in a bathroom stall at work. A night of chardonnay and undercooked chicken casserole.

"I don't like this shade," your co-worker, Gabby, says as she adjusts her lipstick in the mirror. "It's too orange."

It won't matter what shade Gabby paints her mouth. She'll still have a face like a marmoset. Round, close-set eyes. A perpetually furry upper lip. Now she's digging in your purse with her monkey fingers and you can't tell her to stop because your mouth fills with acid and you have to put your head back in the toilet bowl.

"OMG!" You hear her say. "OMG!"

When you look up, she's wagging a pregnancy test in your clammy face. "What's this?"

"I'm not pregnant," you tell Gabby.

"Then why do you have a pregnancy test in your bag?"

You heave again. It's an old test. You forgot it was in there. Your bag is a cornucopia of your life for the last five years. You never clean it out. You never throw anything away.

"Come on," Gabby wheedles. "Take the test. I don't want to audit Mr Wilson yet."

You tug some toilet paper off the roll and wipe your mouth. You flush. You rise shakily to your feet, put your pumps back on, and dust off your pencil skirt. You take the kit from Gabby's hand.

"Fine," you say, closing yourself in the bathroom stall, not sure if you can come up with enough urine when you're this dehydrated.

As you trickle away, Gabby dances outside the stall. A rain dance. The dance of child waiting for ice cream. There hasn't been this much excitement in accounting since the clown hired for Gabby's birthday turned out to be a stripper.

You're not worried about the test. Shaun keeps condoms in your night table drawer. You're lucky. You've been told this many times by many people. So lucky to have a progressive boyfriend who takes responsibility, who buys condoms and wears condoms and never makes a fuss about it. So progressive, in fact, that a week ago Shaun used a female pronoun to refer to his penis. After sex, he turned to you and said, *you really gave her a workout. She won't be ready to go again for hours*. And you said, *what a lazy little bitch*. You haven't returned his calls since.

You hand the damp pregnancy stick to Gabby. You purposely didn't shake it off so that when she brings it to her face, she wrinkles her nose and pee rivulets from her fingers to her blouse sleeve.

You wait. You let her avid marmoset eyes seek the second pink line. You know it's coming. Thorazine always gives you a false positive. That's why pregnancy tests are useless for you. And while it once terrified you, this time it's like a magic trick. A hidden panel in a box that allows you to be sawn in half. A bullet caught in the mouth that's hidden beneath your tongue before the gun even fires its blank shot.

Gabby's jaw drops. She catches your bloodshot eye in the mirror. "OMG," she says. "You're pregnant!"

Okay, maybe you should have corrected her and revealed the pregnancy prank. Or maybe you should have faked a miscarriage. You could have had some sick days. You could have stayed in bed and binge-watched a series or indulged in some online shopping. Maybe a new handbag. Or you could have gone to a casino. Played the slots, got drunk on Mai Tais, slept with a man in a golden thong. But you didn't. Instead, you let the office staff fuss over you with lavender-mint tea and some stupid chakra bracelet that's supposed to prevent morning sickness. You let Gabby plan an elaborate baby shower. You strapped Shaun's bicycle helmet to your stomach every day until your skin became raw and red from the constant pull and tear of the tape.

But you're smart. You learn fast. Pregnancy isn't a medical condition. It's a state of mind. It's a lifestyle choice.

Your father is the easiest to fool. On the screen, he looks about ten years older than the last time you skyped with him.

"You're eating lots of healthy food?" he says.

You pat your protruding belly like it's the result of a large and nutritious meal.

"Getting enough sleep?" he says.

"Eight hours plus," you say.

"You have a good obstetrician?"

"He delivered Kim Kardashian's surrogate's baby," you say. "His name is Psalm. I'm thinking of naming mine Crucifix."

Your father ignores the naming bit. "She's a good friend of yours, this Kardashian girl?"

"We're besties," you say.

As your father nods approval, a lone tuft of hair in the front of his head sways and his face pixelates. You wonder if he has the same lousy view of you. If he can't see the bags under your eyes or your arms hanging like toothpicks from your t-shirt.

"Have you had an ultrasound yet?"

"Yes!" You scramble to grab the ultrasound photo from the coffee table. You downloaded it from an online site for genetic abnormalities. They had the best quality pictures for your printer. You think this might be the foetus with an irregular genome, but, really, who would know from a picture? Your father squints at the screen as you hold up the ultrasound.

"Beautiful!" he declares. He looks so happy, so genuinely pleased to see the glow of foetal life curled inside your womb that you decide to ask.

"I could give you a copy," you say, "if I could come over." There is silence as your father rubs his craggy cheeks. You plunge ahead. "Or we could meet somewhere? A café? You only live a few miles away." It's true. You could walk to your father's condo in thirty minutes. You could probably pick up dinner on the way and still make it there in under an hour.

"The thing is," your father says, then stops and scratches his stubble again. "The thing is, sweetheart, it's just not a good time. Marina and the girls and I are going on vacation next week. There are so many things to do. I'm sure you understand."

Marina is your stepmother. She thinks you're a bad influence ever since you took your twin stepsisters, squealing and snickering, to the roof of your father's condo and dropped the Thanksgiving turkey carcass twenty stories down onto the sidewalk. It didn't land on anyone, but as Marina said, *that is not the point*. You were re-enacting your mother's suicide with holiday leftovers, which was *sick* and *inappropriate* and made you an *unstable person*.

Now your throat's gone dry. The ultrasound falls to the floor, though you won't realise this until later when you find it ripped from being trod upon. "Where are you going on vacation?" you croak.

As your father rattles on about the South of France, you realise all the questions he asked came from his experience with Marina. Your father didn't concern himself with diet and sleep and obstetrics until Marina's geriatric pregnancy seven years ago. He went to all the appointments and all the classes with her. He took Lamaze and claimed he never really breathed until he met Marina.

"How is Shaun?" he asks.

"He's in the South of France," you say.

Your father's features once again pixelate so that he seems light years away, deployed to a different planet. This time his voice cuts in and out. "… such a great guy… so lucky to have him…"

You squat in front of the laptop, willing your father to rematerialize, to ask you more questions about your pregnancy. Baby names or baby registries or a birth plan. Then your father's picture miraculously clears. The static evaporates from his voice. "Your mother," he says, "would have been over the moon."

Your throat tightens. You blink back tears. You imagine your mother floating somewhere over the moon, weightless, soaring over craters and sand dunes of moon dust, her body defying gravity in a way it never did on earth.

In the background, you hear a door open and close. Your stepsisters are giggling. There is a command to remove shoes. Marina is home. Your father whispers at the screen, "Got to go, sweetheart. Take care of yourself."

Before the laptop goes dark, Marina appears in the living room, a long spidery woman with dyed black hair. She is loaded down with shopping bags. Probably beach towels and sunscreen and sandals and matching floppy hats for the whole family. Travel size shampoos and hand sanitisers and antacids for all the *fromage* and *fruits de mer* and *vin rouge*. You wish you could take a trip like them, except to the moon, to visit your mom.

"Should I go with a pink or blue theme for the baby shower?" Gabby has one buttock perched on your desk. She holds a notebook in one hand and a pen in the other like she's waiting to take your order at a restaurant, a dingy one where waitresses rest their asses on tables.

"Can it be space-themed?" you say. "Like outer space? Like the moon?"

"Hmmm." Gabby bounces the pen against her pursed lips. "I think space is a theme for a birthday party, not a baby shower."

You stare at your computer screen. Marina has sent you an email with pictures from *La Grande Plage*. Your half-sisters are indeed wearing the floppy hats you imagined. Your father has rejected the hat and turned a nut brown. Marina still looks like a spider in a string bikini.

"Are you saying you want a gender-neutral baby shower?" Gabby says. "That is so progressive. Did Shaun suggest that?"

You delete Marina's email. Then you delete all your unanswered emails until your inbox is a clean white space.

"Leave it to me," Gabby says. "I will throw the perfect gender-neutral shower!"

*

Shaun is waiting when you get home. Since you threw his key into the storm sewer, he stands outside your apartment every day with a bouquet of Shasta daisies.

"You're glowing," he says.

"I'm an atomic blast," you say. "I could melt your face off."

"Are you taking your medication?" he asks.

"Are you?" you say, even though you know Shaun only takes mugwort capsules to boost his Chi.

"You're still on Thorazine?" he says.

You lumber towards him. You have a practiced pregnancy gait now. You're in week 28 and your pelvis has expanded to accommodate the baby's growing head, so you walk with a bow-legged waddle. Shaun takes your arm and guides you up the steps to your apartment.

"I'm not supposed to take it," you say. "I'll give birth to a retard or a freak."

This is what Kate from HR told you. She came into the bathroom shortly after Gabby's *OMG you're pregnant!* proclamation and immediately spotted the bottle of Thorazine in your open purse. She snatched it out, her manicured nails sharpened to Nosferatu points, and squinted at the label.

You can't take these when you're pregnant, she said. *Your baby could grow an extra arm. Or gills.* Then she flushed your medication down the toilet. *You can thank me later,* she added, *when you don't have to wheel your fourth grader into school wearing a bib and a diaper.*

You didn't argue. You never needed the pills, anyway. Shaun was the only one who insisted you did. And your dad.

Now your ex-boyfriend paces in front of you, his brow furrowed. Handsome in jeans and a suffrage heroes trailblazer t-shirt. A fistful of Shasta daisies wilting in his hand.

"That's not true," he says. "I talked to an obstetrician. She said the possibility of having a special needs baby is low, even if you're taking anti-psychotics."

God, how you hate those words. *Special needs. Anti-psychotic.* You wish you had his key back so you could throw it in the sewer again. "I'm not letting you in," you say.

"I don't think you should be alone," he says. "It's not safe. What if something goes wrong? What if you need help?"

"I'm safe," you say. "I bought a gun. Guess what kind?"

Shaun stares down at his Birkenstocks and rubs his eyebrows in a pained way.

"It's a revolver," you say. "I sleep with it under my pillow. Like in the old noir movies."

"I miss you," Shaun says. "Tell me you don't really have a gun."

You won't admit it, but you miss Shaun too. His assortment of condoms and power bars in the night table drawer, his soft snoring, his sandalwood smell on your bath towels and bedsheets. When you ripped the helmet from your flat, chafed belly last night, one of Shaun's sandy hairs floated out and landed on the bathroom tiles. You picked it up, turned it this way and that in the halogen light, and put it back inside the helmet. It seemed important somehow that Shaun's DNA be involved in the pregnancy.

"Can I at least look for my bicycle helmet?" he says. "I bought a new one, but that one was my lucky helmet."

Shaun's bicycle helmet, the one now hidden between the two of you under a woollen sweater dress, is indeed lucky. A year ago, Shaun was sideswiped by a door-dash driver. He flew through the air on a busy thoroughfare and landed, headfirst, on the pavement. Later, over shared salmon rolls and shrimp tempura, gratis the guilty door dash driver, you and Shaun examined the helmet, awed by the absence of any chips or cracks. The only sign that there had been an accident was a small scuff mark near the base.

"All right," you say. "You've got five minutes."

He follows you down the hallway to your apartment. Once you get inside, it's stifling. So much hotter than outside. You didn't leave any windows open or fans blowing to combat the autumn heatwave. You can almost see steam rising from the dirty laundry that covers your entire floor. You don't like to touch soiled clothing, and since Shaun was the one who always took the laundry downstairs or to the laundromat, it's accumulated in giant heaps ever since he left. Your solution is to order a new outfit each morning online. Overalls and rompers and dresses. The key is to find a maternity garment that can't be lifted by a nosy co-worker who wants to inspect your bare belly. The outfit is always delivered the night before, waiting neatly inside a box that you pay extra to have gift wrapped.

While Shaun steps gingerly over balled-up flower-print dresses and front-tie dresses and t-shirt dresses, you make a beeline for the bathroom. You must make sure the tape and bandages are hidden deep inside the overflowing trash bin. The used tampons, too. Then you look in the mirror, smooth your hair back into a chignon, and roll on some lip gloss and deodorant. When you come out, Shaun's sitting on the bed. He can't take his eyes off the piles and piles of dirty laundry.

"I could run downstairs and throw in a load," he says. "It would only take a minute."

"No need," you say, kicking a mound into the corner to clear a path. "Once the baby comes, I'm going to gather it all into trash bags and drop it off at Goodwill."

He picks up a purple silk tunic. It hangs from his finger like a drop of paint. "Is this real silk? It must have cost a fortune."

"My dad is paying for it all. He insisted. He's really excited to be a grandfather."

Shaun looks doubtful but says nothing. He knows Marina manages your father's finances. He also knows Marina hates you. He was there for the turkey carcass incident on Thanksgiving. While he didn't defend your behaviour, you could tell he thought Marina was a flaming bitch.

"Does it kick yet?" he asks, dropping the tunic and gesturing at your belly.

You know from the wimpled midwife on the pregnancy app that the baby can start kicking as early as 16 weeks. "Of course," you say, "it kicks all the time. It's a fucking Rockette."

"Can I feel it?"

"No."

Shaun's face sags. "You know, it's my baby too."

You start to sweat. The bulk of the sweater dress that made you feel safe earlier today is now roasting you alive, the heat clawing around your neck and spiralling under the bicycle helmet so that your torso feels engulfed by an inferno. A sheen of sweat covers your entire body. The tissues you stuffed into your bra to make your breasts look swollen are now sodden and crumbling inside the hollowing cups.

"You look sexy," Shaun says, shifting tactics. He makes a space for you to sit next to him on the unmade bed. You do. Your shoulders touch. Then your hands. You radiate heat. You think you may spontaneously combust. Then he kisses you, softly, the way you like. And you don't combust. You melt. He kisses you again and runs his hands down your neck to the small of your back, then inches them toward your stomach. You leap away.

"Don't touch me," you say.

"What?"

Your mind goes blank. What can you possibly tell him? Shaun is sprawled on your bed, looking baffled and fit. You notice he has opened a window and put the Shasta daisies in a vase nearby. The petals flutter in the breeze. It must have been while you were in the bathroom. He also began separating the whites from the darks into two massive piles of laundry. What a thoughtful and industrious guy. And you want him. You want him so much. Your hips are twitching in the direction of the bed. You're tingling and wet. Not just with sweat, anymore.

"The truth is," you say, stalling, "the truth is, I'm shy about how I look. I feel fat."

"You look beautiful," Shaun says.

"I want to keep my dress on," you say.

If Shaun looks disappointed, it's only for a second. "Sure," he says, "but do you mind if I go commando?"

You shake your head. You don't mind at all. You watch him take off his clothes.

"Totally commando," he laughs. "I don't even have to wear a condom."

You hadn't thought of that. No condom. You make a mental note to buy the morning-after pill. Then you make another mental note not to do that as a visibly pregnant woman.

Shaun takes you in his arms. You rest your hot head on his shoulder, marvel at the way his sweat is cool and sweet, unlike yours, which is sulphurous. Once again, his hands move to your belly. You step back. You can't let him touch you. If he finds out, Shaun is so honest he will make you tell everyone: your co-workers, the credit card company, your dad, and, oh my god, Marina, who will twist up her lips in a spidery smirk. *Sick. Unstable. Just like her mother*. You can't let that happen. You can't. You would rather die. You would rather Shaun die.

You blurt, "Can I tie you up?"

At first, Shaun thinks you're joking, then he says, "For real?"

"It'll be fun," you say, picking up the purple pregnancy tunic from the floor.

Shaun falls backwards obligingly on the bed when you give him a firm shove. He stays hard. This is why you love Shaun. He is unflappable. He places his wrists near the bedpost so you can tie him up easily. You adjust the pillow under his head, so he doesn't feel the butt of the revolver. If he knew about the gun, he may be less game than he is now. As you do these things, your thickly swathed belly hovers over his face. He quick, quick kisses it with a funny smacking sound. He doesn't notice you are completely hollow.

"Do I need a safe word?" he laughs.

You take off your panties and hitch up your sweater dress as far on your hips as you dare. "How about *bicycle helmet*?" you say. Then you climb onto Shaun and guide him inside you.

Maybe the virtual midwife is right about all those pregnancy hormones making you horny as hell. Riding Shaun has always felt good, but this is transcendent. As Shaun bucks beneath you, you start to bounce, faster, then slower, always trying to get the pressure right, the speed right. Sweat runs down your scalp and neck, settles into the creases behind your knees and ankles, pools on Shaun's stomach, soaks your sweater dress until the whole room reeks of wet wool. Your hair comes out of your chignon and clings to your face in wet clumps. You start to shudder inside, and it radiates outward, pulsing in sharp waves that loosen and lower until both you and Shaun cry out simultaneously. And far away, as if from outer space, you hear something fall and hit the floor.

You open your eyes. Your dress is all the way up to your chest. The sweaty straps of tape attached to your stomach flutter in the breeze. Goose bumps cover your scabbed and flattened tummy.

"Bicycle helmet," Shaun says.

You pull down your dress. Your breathing is uneven. Your hands shake. You haven't taken Thorazine in months. You reach beneath the pillow. You pull out the revolver. You know there is a bullet in each of the six chambers in the cylinder. You hold the handle of the gun, lift your arm, and use your thumb to pull the hammer back and cock it. You aim the revolver and let your pointer finger skim the trigger.

"You need help," Shaun whispers, his body absolutely still. "I love you."

You pull the trigger. Nothing happens. You click through each chamber in an increasingly predictable game of Russian roulette. Of course Shaun emptied the gun. He would have done that before separating laundry. Before putting daisies in a vase.

"I love you too," you say.

Two months later, the office workers have tied a yellow bow on your head. The entire baby shower is yellow-themed with suns and daffodils and bumblebees to honour your choice of gender neutrality for your offspring. Your co-workers are at the office on a Saturday afternoon. Normally, they would be nursing hangovers and attending the sports games of their own offspring, but they have gathered today to initiate you into the cult of motherhood. Every one of them is a Juno in jeggings, a Demeter with a diaper bag. They spread their offerings and libations on a long table in the office meeting room: au gratin potatoes, homemade tamales, pasta salad, a fruit and cheese platter, brownies.

You select a flute of champagne and a slice of apple with a thick smear of brie.

"It's a golden shower!" Gabby declares, rolling a Mylar balloon-festooned office chair into the conference room. Your personal dais. Once you're seated, she hands you a small yellow pillow to support your lower back.

You sip champagne. Your lower back feels amazing.

"I brought non-alcoholic mimosas," Kate from HR informs you.

"They're really good," you say.

"That's not what you're drinking," Kate says.

You bat playfully at a lemon-coloured streamer hanging over your head. This is your third champagne flute. Your head is spinning.

"For fuck's sake," Kate says, removing the flute from your fingers and replacing it with a non-alcoholic mimosa. "This isn't France."

Before you're allowed to open your gifts, everyone has to play a series of baby-themed games designed by Gabby. First, there is a relay race from the conference room to the copy machine to the break room and back again as your team carries spoonfuls of banana-plum baby food. There are several *whoops* and *shit*, one crash onto a keyboard, and lots and lots of saucy fruit spilled and pounded into the grey broadloom carpeting, which Gabby leaves for the Sunday cleaning crew.

Then comes a game where everyone must recite a dirty limerick with a pacifier in their mouth. Gabby delivers one about a man from Kent while Brenda from IT recites another about woman from Cape Cod. You make one up about Marina, a woman from France, who never pulls up her pants, and so her only romance is with bats, rats, and cats, who crawl up inside her twat. And because you're tipsy and there's a pacifier in your mouth, you don't judge yourself for using slant rhyme.

The last game involves competitive diaper changing. Gabby has brought a plastic baby doll, a stack of diapers, and a stopwatch. It goes faster and faster with each guest until Kate, who tells everyone she's done this a million times, whips off the diaper in a trice, places a new one beneath the plastic bottom, but before she can adhere the tape, the doll's left leg snaps off in her hand. As everyone laughs, you take the opportunity to sneak some real champagne into your mimosa. When you turn back, the laughter has ceased. Kate's face is poison-apple red.

"That's not fair," she says. "I was the last one up. The doll was already broken before I started." Kate jabs the little leg at Gabby. "I want a new doll. I want a do over."

"Come on," someone says, "the prize is the leftover sheet cake. It doesn't even have a flavour. It just tastes like sugar."

"Hey, my sister made that cake," someone else says. "It's vanilla flavoured."

"I want a new doll." Kate plants her feet and crosses her arms over her chest. You get the impression she has said this before at a different age with parents who probably got the doll ASAP.

Gabby turns whiter than the sheet cake, then Brenda takes the plastic baby leg from Kate's manicured grip. "This would make a decent dildo," she says, "for that woman from Cape Cod."

Everyone laughs again, even Kate this time, and Gabby's eyes tear up with relief.

You are ushered back into the special chair. A gift is placed in your lap, or what's left of your lap, since now your belly rests halfway down your thighs. You tear open the paper to find a box of tea with ingredients that remind you of a bad camping trip: thistle and rue and stinging nettle.

A woman who works in the sales department tells you the tea works miracles with breast milk. "At first it was a sad little trickle," she says, "but after a cup of that tea, it was like someone nicked my carotid artery. It sprayed everywhere. Milk, that is, not blood."

You open a series of boob-themed gifts: pumps and special bras and creams and burp cloths and a pop up tent for when you have to feed your gender neutral offspring in public. The champagne helps you fake enthusiasm, but when Gabby squeals, you fumble a jar of lanolin and it joins the banana mush on the carpet.

"It's time!" Gabby yodels.

Kate appears with a giant gift-wrapped box, and soon all the women are clapping and whistling and hooting with excitement. You think maybe the box is a ruse and Gabby rehired the stripper-clown that performed at her birthday party, but, no, the racket is about the gift.

"This is the big one," Gabby says.

"From the people in corporate," Kate adds.

You wonder what it could be. A car seat? A car? A trip to France where you can drink without shame and kick sand into Marina's botoxed face? As you tear open the shiny paper, you're giddy, you're all smiles, you're five years old again and it's a Christmas morning and your mother has remembered what you asked Santa for all those months ago. Your mother always remembered.

"OMG!" Gabby says. "It's a Chick&Chat!"

The cover of the box features a pregnant woman in pastel yoga pants, whose head is not in the frame, but who wears what appears to be a white tube top around her pregnant belly. With one elegant hand, she holds up her iPhone. Without a head, it's hard to gauge her reaction to what she's looking at on the iPhone, but it must be good because her other hand rests tranquilly on her perfectly rounded belly.

"I always wanted one." Kate runs her fingers reverently over the box.

"I heard they cost as much as a Bengal tiger cub," Gabby says.

A box cutter tears into the tape and hands rip apart cardboard, removing the tube top and instructional manual.

"It's the latest in biometric pregnancy monitoring," Brenda reads. "It doesn't just give the baby's vital signs, it registers the baby's kicks, its heart rate, and all uterine contractions to provide the baby with a voice. It's the most advanced method of foetus/mother communication in the world. And it's BPA free."

"My sister-in-law has one," says the woman with arterial boobs. "She and her baby were having full conversations before the baby was even born. Full conversations!" She lowers her voice. "It turned out the baby was a Green Party voter."

"You download the app that connects to the device," Brenda says. "It's easy. I can do it for you."

Reluctantly, you hand Brenda your phone after you're sure you've deleted every worried and angry text Shaun has sent since you made love and pulled the trigger.

"Put it on," Gabby says, starting a chorus of *put it on, put it on* like a drinking game at a hen party and you shrink inside your corduroy romper. You're grateful you sprung for the silicone pad to cover the bicycle helmet, but still, one good groping from a baby shower attendee and the gig is up.

You lurch to your feet, light-headed, and stumble away from the pile of boob gifts and chanting women. "I'll put it on in the bathroom," you say.

"I'll come with you," Gabby says. "It'll be like when we found out you were pregnant!"

Gabby trails you to the bathroom where you close yourself in the same stall you were puking in months ago. You think you may puke now. You're caught. You can't make a run for it with Gabby outside the door. So, you unbuckle your romper and take the pregnancy monitoring tube top when Gabby flings it over the top of the stall. You wrap it tightly around your belly and secure the Velcro. "All set," you say, praying the app will be silent and everyone will think your baby is dead.

When you and Gabby emerge from the bathroom, Brenda has the app hooked up to the office computer system, so all the women at the baby shower can see and hear your womb projected on a screen and through the speaker system. It's like a giant ultrasound PowerPoint presentation.

"Say something," Brenda says.

You wave at the screen. "Hello," you say.

"Address the baby, not the screen," Kate instructs.

You gaze down at your stomach, at the palimpsest of bicycle helmet and tape and silicone pad and biometric tube top. "Hello," you say again.

"Maybe you need an ice-breaker," Gabby suggests. "How about, if the baby could travel anywhere, where would the baby go?"

You repeat Gabby's ice breaker, cooing as you ask the baby where it would go, if it could go anywhere in the world, no, anywhere in the universe. Suddenly, Brenda points at the screen and all the guests *ooo* and *ahhh*. You watch streaks of light jet across the dark screen like comets or shooting stars.

"OMG!" Gabby shrieks.

Two more shooting stars flash across the screen, dovetailing around each other like an electrified double helix. But you don't *ooo* and *ahhh* with the other women because this is exactly how space would look if you were sitting on the moon. Which is where your mother is, which is where your baby wants to travel, which is where you will all come together.

You unhook your romper. You place your hands beneath the tube top and reach down past the tape, past the helmet, until you hit warm skin. Then you feel it. A mound, small but firm, the satellite that's been orbiting you for months now.

SHANNON SCOTT is an adjunct Professor of English at several Twin Cities universities. She has contributed short fiction to Nightscript, Coppice and Brake: A Dark Fiction Anthology, *and* Oculus Sinister. *She has also published essays on wolves and werewolves in collections from Manchester University Press. She was co-editor of* Terrifying Transformations: An Anthology of Victorian Werewolf Fiction, 1838-1896.

ONE FOR SORROW

Adam Down

Vincent frowned at the magpie on his workbench. It hadn't been there last night; he was sure of it. Even on the worst mornings, when the brain fog settled over his mind like a pall, he remembered all of his creations vividly. And the stuffed bird perched on the varnished mahogany block was not one of them.

It sat amongst his other avian specimens, between a starling with the top of its skull removed, still waiting for Vincent's special finishing touch, and two sparrows on a tree branch. The magpie's iridescent feathers, so black they seemed edged with blue, shone in the sunlight filtering in through the workshop window.

He reached for the magpie, half expecting it to shake itself awake and fly away. Feathers rustled beneath his fingers. The skin beneath felt warm, almost alive.

Could someone have bought it for him, perhaps? His nephew, Scott, sometimes turned up with some threadbare cat he'd found in an antique shop, or a boss-eyed squirrel from one of the house clear-outs he performed for the council. Vincent would always thank him, then hide whatever Scott had given him in the closet the moment he left.

He didn't understand that for Vincent, the joy of taxidermy lay as much in the process as the final result. All the methodical, fine detail work, infusing something worn out and lost with a semblance of its former life. He loved the glassy-eyed simulacra that were the fruits of his hours of painstaking labour. They were works of art, straight from his heart.

The pieces Scott picked up for him were poor, lumpy things, amateurish most of the time. Sometimes they weren't even genuine taxidermy jobs, just bad fakes made of metal and plastic struts and cheap, synthetic fur. Even the best example Scott had ever found—a pine martin with its front paws on a section of natural deadfall—paled in comparison to the magpie.

Not Scott, then. *So you did it. You just forgot about it.* The idea formed in his head like an iceberg in a shipping lane, not too horrible on the surface, but brimming with unseen menace.

You're losing your mind. You're going like Trudy. You'll be dribbling into your muesli by this time next year. Vincent shuddered. Though his wife lived on, dementia had robbed them both of everything that made her special. He still loved her, but every visit to her room up in the attic conversion left him melancholy. It was a mausoleum to loss, and a promise of what lay in store for him if he went the same way.

Yes, it would be all too easy to convince himself that the magpie was his doing. Of course, there was a simple way to identify whether that was the case. No-one else sliced the top off the specimen's skull as part of the taxidermy process—that was his own personal touch. Well, his and Trudy's really.

He probed the magpie's bullet-shaped head gently with his thumb and forefinger, and there it was. A thin, raised line of glue, all the way around.

Vincent made a small, strangled sound in the back of his throat and put the bird back on his workbench, his hands shaking. He took a deep breath and let it out slowly.

So the bird's one of yours, what of it? You've worked on dozens of pieces over the last couple of years, it's no surprise you forgot one of them. It's nothing. But that didn't explain why it was on the workbench when he came in. He must have put it there. Who else could have? Trudy?

He laughed at the thought, and didn't like the slight hysterical edge he heard in it at all. He needed to do something normal, something to focus his mind. The starling still needed finishing off, maybe he could get lost in his work for a while. But that meant visiting Trudy first.

Vincent stood, his back popping, and left the magpie on his workbench. The stairs to the attic were narrow and dark, but he took them easily enough. Even his hip stayed silent, as if to highlight that his body was ready and willing to outlive his mind whether he liked it or not.

"Afternoon, dear," he said.

Trudy lay motionless on the bed, a skeleton in human skin, her skull wrapped in a thick layer of surgical gauze. Eyes—a brilliant blue that had set his heart aflutter the first time he'd seen them—stared off in different directions, the skin around them slack and bruised. She was surrounded by machines and drips. An intravenous tube fed her, and a catheter linked to a bag dealt with most of the waste. Another drip sent a steady dose of antibiotics through her bloodstream. He'd feared he would have to risk using his old contacts at the hospital to source it all, but he hadn't needed to. Amazing what you could buy on the internet nowadays, and how few questions were asked.

The bandages wrapped around her misshapen head were sodden with yellow and grey liquid, and a little had leaked out onto the stack of pillows propping her up.

"You've been trying to move again, haven't you? What have I told you about that? You'll lose what little brain you have left."

Oh well, he needed to remove the bandages to finish the starling, anyway. He unwrapped her head carefully, discarding the soaked wadding and antiseptic wipes packed beneath. The top of her head yawned open, a large portion of the skull removed. That was in the wardrobe somewhere, unless he'd forgotten where he'd put that too. The pinkish grey of her brain glistened, still quivering slightly from his gentle unpacking. Most of the frontal and parietal lobes were gone, already implanted in the skulls of his taxidermies downstairs, but there was plenty left.

"Everyone thinks you're dead, dear. You have been really, these last few years. It's for the best. They couldn't possibly stand to see you like this, but I'll be here until the end."

Vincent pulled on a pair of disposable gloves, and rummaged around in the bedside table drawer. Pulling out a new syringe, he tore it from its packaging and injected the painkillers into her neck. Of course he knew that the brain had no nerves of its own, no way of feeling or communicating pain, but he did it for Trudy. He didn't want to hurt her.

It was incredibly unfair, how the dementia had robbed him of his wife. Her sense of humour went first, then her speech, then her personality. Within a year of diagnosis Trudy had been reduced to following him around the house like a lost lamb, slack-jawed and vacant. What kind of life was that for someone he'd once watched can-canning across their bedroom in nothing but a sparkly top hat and a mischievous grin? That was when he'd decided to find a way for her to live on.

The scalpel was on the surgical steel tray next to the bed—at least that hadn't gone walkabout. Vincent picked it up and held it between his thumb and index finger, a practiced motion honed over five decades as a neurosurgeon. His worries about his own mind melted away as he bent over Trudy's cerebral cortex. This was his element.

"You know, I was worried I was losing it earlier on. Bloody magpie, appearing from nowhere. One for sorrow, isn't that how the rhyme goes?" He chatted to Trudy as he sliced into her brain, paring off a thin pink sliver, small enough to fit in the starling's tiny skull. "But visiting you has made me feel much better. You always know how to put my mind at rest."

When he was done, he re-applied the wadding and bandages, and replaced the soiled pillows with clean ones. He lay her back down gently and pulled the covers up to her middle. Vincent took one of her shrivelled claw hands in his and kissed it.

"I will preserve you, my love."

He brushed her slack cheek with his lips and gave her hand one final squeeze. He scooped the piece of brain up from the tray and dropped it into a zip-lock bag filled with ice from the mini freezer beneath the bed. Cerebrum spoiled quickly, and letting it go stale before implanting it would make a mockery of trying to keep what little of Trudy remained.

The magpie wasn't in the workshop when he went back downstairs.

Vincent blinked. The magpie was still gone, but that was a good thing. Maybe it was off trying to find a friend; one for sorrow, two for joy. Yes, that would be much better.

He tried to get down to work, but he couldn't concentrate. The sliver of brain would not play ball, writhing and bucking in the tweezers whenever he tried to fold it into the starling's brain-pan. He re-bagged it and put it in the kitchen freezer to stop it from going off. There was plenty more left before he needed to make any decisions about the parts that dealt with organ function and her central nervous system, but that was no reason to be wasteful.

He found the bird a few hours later, perched on the kitchen breakfast bar. There was no chance of any more work after that.

Vincent turned away, took his overcoat from the hook by the door and shrugged it over his shoulders. A walk would clear his head, and if it didn't, a quick stop at the Dog and Lamppost would.

*

The magpie wasn't in the kitchen when he got home. The breakfast bar was a blank slate in the deepening twilight, a few bits of unread post all that marred its surface. Vincent checked the stools and the floor, in case the thing had fallen somehow, but nothing. It was gone.

That's it. You're going just like her. You don't have a clue where you put it before you went out, do you? And don't try the drinking excuse, you've only had a single whiskey.

He shook his head. No, he would not go like Trudy, he couldn't. Who would look after her if something happened to him? And what would they say about the little matter of his home surgeries? Even if he was in mental decline, that wouldn't be enough to keep him out of prison. So no, he would not go senile. He wouldn't allow it.

Vincent smiled to himself, happy to have come to a decision. There must be a sensible explanation for the day's events somewhere, he just had to find it, and he'd start by finding that damn bird. It was probably in his workshop, where it should be.

He got as far as the doorway and stopped. His breath caught in his throat. Other than a litter of tools, his workbench was empty. The sparrows, the squirrel, the owls, even the unfinished starling—they were all gone.

Vincent stood in the dark, wide-eyed. His grip tightened, convulsing around the doorknob. Without it he might have fallen right there. A heavy ball of dread formed in the pit of his stomach.

The doors of his display cases hung open. For a lingering moment he couldn't will himself to move, and, when the spell finally broke, he staggered across the room like he was on the deck of a sinking ship. The ball in his stomach rolled.

The cases were all empty too. Nearly a hundred pieces gone, vanished into thin air. Only the locked cupboard full of Scott's well-meaning rubbish was undisturbed.

What in god's name was happening? As much as he didn't want to entertain the possibility, he could believe he'd been moving the magpie himself. But all of his taxidermies at once? Not possible. He briefly considered a burglary, but that was ludicrous. The door had been locked when he came home, and he never opened any windows when it was chilly outside. In any case, what kind of robber would take his taxidermies but not the TV downstairs?

A muffled thump sounded from the floor above.

Trudy's room.

The hairs on the back of Vincent's neck stood on end. Slowly and deliberately, he took a small bone saw—the closest thing he had to a weapon—from the workbench and turned, half-expecting someone to be waiting in the doorway. There was no-one.

He scaled the stairs to the attic, his heart thudding harder with every step. The door to Trudy's room was wide open, revealing a heavy slab of darkness, a black hole sucking him inexorably forward. Vincent shuffled to the door and grabbed hold of the frame, not wanting to be drawn into the abyss. He stared into the gloom, unable to turn away.

The silhouettes in the shadows were wrong. He crept a shaky hand across the wall and flicked on the light.

They were everywhere. On every available surface.

The dusty dressing table, the tops of the wardrobe, even the threadbare carpet, were covered in his work. An owl stood on the windowsill, amber eyes glaring. The unfinished starling sat on the bedside table amongst the litter of medical supplies, a small grey mass quivering in its open skull. The magpie perched on Trudy's pillow, level with her head.

Every single one was looking at him. Vincent reeled.

Trudy sat up. Her head lolled as she rose, the bandages wrapped around her skull speckling with fresh yellow and grey. Around her, muzzles twitched, eyes blinked, and feathers ruffled as the taxidermies responded to the dark miracle unfolding in their midst.

She stood, head rolling, wasted arms dangling at her sides. The sodden bandage came loose and spattered grey goo across the wall.

For a long moment, the pitter patter of drool and brain fluid on the bare floorboards were the only sounds in the house. Then, Trudy's jaw yawned open, but it was Vincent who screamed.

The bone saw fell from his hand. He sank to his knees, and his creations rose up to meet him.

The last thing he saw, before everything went dark, was the magpie, iridescent wings beating as it flew straight at his head.

ADAM DOWN writes stories about bad people doing bad things, often to one another. His work has appeared across the darkest corners of the internet, including Coffin Bell Journal, Friday Flash Fiction, *and* Tales from the Menagerie. *He resides in the UK, where he does in fact know a taxidermist. Adam has seen parts of a crow that he never knew existed, and would have preferred it to stay that way. You can find him on Twitter @AdamDownFiction.*

THE DARK GIFT

Joshua Robinson

The full moon hung in the sable sky, casting slivers of light on the girl I'd spend forever with. Cherish and love, always. My Cindy Pop, strolling beside me, twigs snapping underfoot as we crossed through the otherwise silent forest.

I found it hard to imagine her freckled face any prettier than it already was. Yet by tonight's end, her beauty would triple—like many other qualities—and it couldn't happen to a more perfect person. A more deserving person.

And she deserved this. I'd never been surer of anything.

"So, what's the surprise?"

I gave her hand a delicate squeeze. "When we get to the lake."

"Fine. Be that way." She shivered. "Man, it's cold."

"Take my jacket."

"Nah, I'll live. But. This does raise an important point, one for future reference. That there are lots of places you can take a girl. Just FYI."

I grinned. "Is that so?"

"Yup."

"And what might those be?"

"Oh, I don't know. The movies, bowling... Spain."

"Ha, Spain? Maybe. There'll be plenty of time for that. For now, though, try and appreciate all this." I gestured to the withered trunks around us and hugged her close.

"Dude. This is like the sixth time you've brought me here. I mean, it's pretty peaceful, but I don't quite get your raging boner."

I snickered. "You should count yourself lucky."

"Lucky, huh?"

"That's right. This is *my* forest. But you keep playing your cards right, and you might just get to move in." I shot her a devilish wink.

That earned me a laugh, a dimpled smile, and best of all, a shoulder punch. Her fist sent tingles rippling across my body. Glorious.

"Dork." She stood on tiptoe and kissed my cheek. "Count yourself lucky that you're a looker."

And to have found you at all, angel. Back at the Haunted Mansion...

I'd hidden between two skeletons, making quick meals of passersby. My last intended victim was a petite redhead, jumping and giggling at the scares while picking at cotton candy. I yanked her into the shadows like the rest, only this one barely yelped or fought. After a stunned pause, she grinned a cheeky grin, and before I could bare my teeth, planted her lips on mine.

"I'm Cindy."

"Uh... okay. I'm—"

She hushed me, pressing two fingers to my lips. "Hot, I know. I'm taking you home."

And that was that.

We stepped out from under the canopy and onto the stony shore. The black lake shimmered and stretched before us, a silent witness to the coming miracle. The stage was set. The moment, perfect. And the memories we'd make, imminently, ones that not even millennia could hope to obliterate.

"Awww." Cindy approached the lake before spinning around to face me, a hand over her heart. "You got me a body of water? You shouldn't have."

I rolled my eyes then chased her, wet stones crunching beneath our feet. After scooping her up like the babe she was, I twirled once, twice, her arms around my neck as she snorted with joy.

"Stooop!"

"Oh." I stopped. "Fancy a swim?"

"No. Put me down."

"As you wish."

Cindy slipped from my arms, then straightened out her denim skirt. "Where's the surprise at?" She folded her arms, all business.

A rare shudder jolted down my spine at an outcome I'd never considered: Cindy saying no. Running for the hills, even. What then?

"Well?"

"Yeah, I… gimme a sec."

She stepped up to me and took my hands. The scent of maraschino cherry filled my nose. "Relax."

"Okay." I inhaled deep, then let a heavy breath pass my lips. Here goes. "I've been thinking about this since the day we met. Since the moment you ate my face."

"You started it."

"Yeah, I guess that's true. But I'm so glad I did. Because you're exactly what I've sought my entire, lonely life."

She bit her lip. "Craig…"

I brushed her hair behind her ear; caressed her tender cheek with my palm. "We've been together, what, six months? I don't care. That's long enough to know that I need you by my side. From now until whatever end awaits us. That's why I have to confess…" I paused.

"Confess what?"

Her bottom lip had twitched at the word, and in that scintilla of a second, an image flickered behind those sapphire eyes. One I didn't recognise.

"Babe?"

I focused my sight, muting the extraneous, and scoured her soul for that which surfaced.

No, that's not—it can't be.

Cindy was on all fours, taking it from behind. Moaning. Sweating. Bed rocking. A man pumping and thrusting… but it wasn't me. That *wasn't me.*

I shrank back. My stomach heaved.

"What's wrong?"

"You fucked him."

Her face stiffened. Heartbeat quickened. Saliva slid down her throat in a squelching swallow. "I don't... how—"

"You fucked him and you loved it. Like a tramp. A whore."

"Hey, fuck you," she spat. "And whatever goddamn game you're playing." She stormed off toward the forest. "Shove your surprise up your ass!"

I doubled over, sucking in the bitter air as fast as I expelled it. Cindy was never going to tell me, was she? And to think how close I came. To granting the Dark Gift. Eternal life. Turning her! That filthy, lying—fury exploded within me, bursting from my lips in a guttural growl that rippled the water and shook the branches for miles. "You were so perfect."

A scream stabbed my eardrums.

From beyond the trees.

Cindy's.

I arrived in seconds. She had her back to a tree, jerking her head in all directions as she scanned the surrounding darkness.

She caught sight of me. "Craig."

"What is it?"

"Bats. One flew right at me. Just came out of nowhere."

I opened my mouth, but couldn't speak another word. Not with splinters puncturing my heart. Crippling me. The clapping of foreign flesh against hers, reverberating in my ears—the image carved into my skull. Then it came to me, the truth of truths. That maybe she had earned a gift after all.

"Look," she said. "I'm so sorry. Walk back with me, we'll talk. About everything. Promise."

Everything's ruined. You're ruined. "Sure."

She wrapped her arms around me, sniffling into my chest. "I love you. It was one time. We weren't even official yet."

"Shh, now."

"You're the best thing that's ever happened to me. I won't lose you. I won't."

"It's okay." *It's all over now.*

Cindy leaned back and wiped her eyes. "How'd you even know?"

"Don't worry. That's behind us."

I leaned in, kissed her lips, her cheek, her neck. Every hair stood erect on my body as my fangs slid out from my gums.

"God." She chuckled. "You're freezing. Let's go home first—" She shrieked and fell back onto the floor, grasping at her neck. "The fuck! You bit me."

A toothy grin crossed my face. "Just a taste."

Her lips quivered and her eyes bulged with terror.

I took one step forward, two, three.

She shuffled back on the heels of her hands, kicking at leaves and dirt and twigs.

"Your… your eyes. *Your eyes.*"

I stopped and raised a hand to the sky, embracing the rapid heartbeats of my winged friends. Glorious. "Oh, how you'll moan!"

"What?" Tears streaked down her cheeks; snot ran from nose to lip. A face melting apart, a mask falling loose. "What's even happening right now! Craig? *Craig?*"

"To new beginnings."

I threw down my arm and a legion of bats blitzed from the trees—screeching a sinister symphony—and swarmed the helpless whore. Their crimson eyes glowed with feral hunger as they gnawed on her lips, ripped her cheeks, burrowed between her bloody breasts, leaving not a single inch untouched, and filling the air with sweet, orgasmic iron.

Cindy writhed. Her screams came to a gurgling halt.

There goes her throat. Fangtastic.

She deserved this. I'd never been surer of anything.

JOSHUA ROBINSON is a horror writer living in London, England. He is currently working on an erotic horror novella. His work has been published in Coffin Bell Journal, Night Picnic Journal, *and* Tales to Terrify Podcast, *among others. You can find him on Instagram @joshua_robinson_author.*

LILAC WINE

Antonia Rachel Ward

The gates are closed to the night. Dense foliage presses against the tarnished iron, green vines intertwining with the dull scrolls. The house stands on a slight rise in the grounds, the grey tiles of its rooftop just visible above the trees. I reach into my pocket for a square of paper, unfolding it to read the scrawled address for the dozenth time. There can be no doubt that this is the right place.

There's no buzzer or intercom, and so, after a moment's hesitation, I push at the gate, forcing it open just far enough for me to slip into the overgrown garden. What once was a drive has long since been overtaken by weeds and brambles. Some of the snarls are as high as my head, and I pick my way through them in the weak moonlight, thorns scratching at my face and hands.

Strange place to hold a party, I think, as I finally emerge from the tangle. Perhaps it's a murder mystery of some sort. All I know is that they want a pianist. It's not often I get a paid gig. Can't look a gift horse in the mouth. Lara, my—well, I guess I have to call her my *ex-girlfriend*, now—never believed I could make anything of myself as a musician. I suppose it's a bit late to be trying to prove her wrong, but here I am, nonetheless.

The house has an air of faded grandeur, paint peeling from the timber panelling. Ivy has claimed more than half its façade, and I have to duck beneath the clinging tendrils to get to the door. If this is a murder mystery, they're certainly going all out for atmosphere. This place looks as though it hasn't been lived in for decades.

To my surprise, the door is ajar. It swings open at my touch, and I step into the darkened hallway. Only moonlight illuminates the tiled floor and the sweeping staircase beyond.

"Hello?" My voice withers in the thick silence, and immediately I feel stupid. Of course this is the wrong place. There's nobody here. But as I turn to leave, there's a flicker of movement at the top of the stairs.

"I'll be down in just a moment." A woman's voice, graceful and lilting, with a cut-glass accent. "Do have a drink while you wait."

Near the base of the staircase stands a table I haven't noticed before, a decanter and two glasses on top. Thinking I may as well take advantage of the hospitality, I pour myself a measure of red wine. In the pale light it has a purplish tinge to it, and when I lift it to my lips, the floral aroma is almost overpowering. The taste is heady and sweet, almost cloying, but the more I drink, the more I enjoy it. A sense of calm spreads through me, warm gold flowing to the tips of my fingers.

A footstep on the stairs startles me out of my reverie. The owner of the beautiful voice makes her way down towards me, her gait slow and easy, red-nailed fingers grazing the banister. Her gown is made from purple lace, fragile train pooling on the floor behind her with every step. Her skin is china white, flawless; her face as perfect as a doll's, with rose pink lips and a dark, haughty gaze. Atop her sable hair she wears a crown of lilacs.

I stare at her, dumbfounded, until she reaches the bottom of the stairs and holds out one delicate hand to me.

"Ava," she says, with a smile that shatters my heart in a flash of white teeth. I take her hand and hope never to let it go again.

"I'm Will. You, um… You wanted a pianist?"

"That's right." Ava turns away in a swoosh of skirts, picking up the decanter and the other wine glass. I follow her as she sweeps through to the next room, a small parlour lit by a few flickering candles.

"Great. Well, maybe I could start setting up…" I spot a grand piano in the corner and take a seat, rummaging in my bag for my sheet music.

"Play me something," Ava says, her voice eager. Hungry.

"Now?"

"Please."

I select a piece—something slow and gentle that seems to suit the moment—and as I play, Ava pours me another glass of wine, followed by one for herself. When I finish the tune, she passes me the glass.

"You're very talented," she sighs, leaning on the piano's lid and fixing me with an earnest gaze. "I could listen to you all day."

It feels nice to be recognised for once. Lara never seemed interested in hearing me play, but Ava… well, she's obviously a woman who understands music. A warm swell of pride fills my chest.

"How old are you?" Ava asks as I sip my wine. In the moonlight's pale glow, her perfect visage seems to shimmer, and I wonder whether I've had enough to drink already.

"Twenty-three."

"Oh! You're just a boy!" Ava leans forward and runs the backs of her fingers down my cheek. I bristle—she's surely not *that* much older than me—but I swallow my pride. Which isn't difficult, after all. Not when she's standing so close to me, her dark eyes fixed on mine, filled with a look of sadness and longing that makes me want to reach out and enfold her in my arms. She looks lost, and the thought steals over me that she's been trapped here, alone, for a very long time.

"You're beautiful," I breathe, only dimly aware of what I'm saying.

"How sweet you are." A melancholy smile flits across her face. "*He* was anything but sweet."

"Who?" I follow her gaze to a portrait that hangs over the cold fireplace. A gentleman in a cravat, with dark, furrowed brows. I'm no art historian, but I'm sure that picture must be a couple of hundred years old, at least.

"My husband," she says. "He was a creative man, like you. An artist. He painted that portrait. But his art made him self-absorbed. Or perhaps his self-absorption made him an artist." She sighs. "Who can tell the difference? To be neglected, Will, for some muse—some figment of the imagination—is the worst thing a woman can endure. Like being locked inside a glass coffin, wilting while the world passes by."

"I can't imagine that any man could possibly neglect *you*," I say, with a vehemence that surprises me.

"And yet, you men only love what you can't have. Isn't that right? The moment you have us, you forget why you wanted us in the first place."

"No, I..." I begin, but Ava isn't listening. Her eyes are locked on the painting, and a sudden wave of jealousy seizes me, my blood rushing at the idea of some other man being on her mind. *I* want to be all she thinks of. *I* want to be everything to her. For a moment, the desire to possess her is overwhelming. Bewildered, I take another sip of wine to settle myself.

"Why don't we take a walk?" Ava opens the patio doors and drifts outside. When I follow, I'm surprised to find myself in a carefully tended garden. A grove of lilac trees. The clouds have dispersed, and the full moon picks out the edges of the leaves in a sheen of silver. It even feels warm. Far warmer than it should on an April night.

Ava wanders into the heart of the lilac grove, the flowers of her headdress blending with those hanging from the trees.

"Beautiful, aren't they?" she calls to me. "My lilacs? They only blossom for one night a year. It takes a special fertiliser to give them their magic."

The wine makes my head spin; a rainbow of colours glitters over the scene like light refracted through a crystal. When Ava beckons me to join her, I don't hesitate. She takes a deep draught of wine as I approach, and looks up at me with glistening eyes.

"There you are," she whispers. I can't shake the feeling that she's not looking *at* me, but through me, somehow. To somebody else.

"The wine…" I begin, stupidly.

"Made from the lilac flowers. It helps you see what you want to see." Ava comes closer, lacing her arms around my neck. "Let's not talk."

When she kisses me, the sweetness of the wine mingles with the sour taste of her lips. The scent of the lilacs presses heavy on my thoughts. My mind is a haze: all I know is that I want her. I wrap my arms around her waist, drawing her closer. Where her skin touches mine, my nerves flare like fireworks.

Ava breaks away, tears running down her cheeks. "You left me," she whispers. When I try to reply, she presses a finger against my lips. "Shh… I want to believe."

She doesn't see me. It's him she's thinking of. Whoever *he* is. I should still be jealous, but my thoughts slip away like silk through my fingers. All that matters is the here and now. This moment. Her lips. Her flesh. She slips her dress off, letting it fall to the ground, revealing an expanse of ivory skin too perfect to be real.

With a devilish smile, Ava takes my hand, drawing me over to one of the trees, pulling me down to the ground near its roots. Straddling me, she unzips my fly, and I reach for her, caressing her collarbones, running my fingers down to her breasts. Some small part of my mind resists, telling me something isn't right, but I push the thought away. If this is wrong, I don't care.

Ava takes me inside of her, and I let out a moan. My senses are on edge; I feel delirious. There is nothing in this world except me and her, and the slow motion of her body on top of mine.

"You left me," she says again, her voice sharper this time, somewhere between delight and despair. She arches her back, sucking in her breath through her teeth. "You left me!"

She leans forward, hair brushing my face as she kisses me.

"It's been so long, lover," she whispers. "So long. And I still can't forget you."

I breathe in her lilac scent and hold my breath, hanging on the edge of ecstasy, trying to prolong the moment as much as I can. Somewhere buried deep within the enchanted haze of my thoughts is the certainty that this instant is infinitely precious—a gem I will never grasp again.

"I love you," I blurt. And I mean it, with every fibre of my being.

"No." Ava starts to move again, writhing slowly. Her voice is low, almost threatening. "No, you never did. I was nothing to you." She lets out a gasp. "Nothing!"

Her face contorts, pleasure and fury deforming her porcelain features. The red streak of her lips grows wider. Her eyes sink into darkened sockets. My heart pounds for altogether different reasons. I blink, and she is back to herself, but panic has already set in. My stomach twists. My flesh crawls, cold sweat beading on my brow.

I try to struggle, but Ava holds me firm. Pinning my arms above my head, she lunges for my throat. As her teeth sink into my neck, she lets out a muffled howl. When she draws back, blood streams from her mouth, down her throat, over her breasts. *My* blood.

Pain sears through my consciousness, blasting away the last of the illusion. The night is freezing, the ground hard against my back. And Ava... My God, *Ava*. Her face is changing, her skin tearing, great gashes appearing in her flesh to reveal the black, leathery skin of a corpse. Her mouth splits into a beak-like grin; sharp talons dig into my wrists.

"Blood and bone," she hisses, great, leathery wings extending out from the ripped skin of her shoulders. "Feed my garden. Blood and bone, and the hearts of men."

Her eyes are nothing but empty sockets, infinite and merciless. With one final inhuman cry, she falls upon me. Devours me, teeth tearing through flesh. *Blood and bone, and the hearts of men.*

Somewhere beyond the mist of agony, I hear the iron gates clank shut once more.

ANTONIA RACHEL WARD is an author of horror, gothic and speculative fiction based in Cambridgeshire, UK. Her short stories and flash fiction have been published by Ghost Orchid Press, Black Hare Press, and Quantum Shorts.

ROSALBA

Matias Travieso-Diaz

O Lola c'hai di latti la cammisa / si bianca e russa comu la cirasa,
Quannu t'affacci fai la vucca a risa, / biatu pìlu primu cu ti vasa!
Ntra la puorta tua lu sangu è spasu / ma nun me mpuorta si ce muoru accisu...
E si ce muoru e vaju 'n paradisu / si nun ce truovo a ttia, mancu ce trasu.
(O Lola, your dress is white as milk, / You are white and red like a cherry,
Your lips smile when you look through the window, / Blessed is he who gives
you the first kiss!
Your threshold is sprinkled with blood, / And I don't care if I'm killed there.
And if I die and go to Paradise, / If I don't find you there, I will not even enter.)
—Pietro Mascagni, Cavalleria Rusticana, Scene 1.

I leave home at daybreak. I get on the dirt road by the hut and go on a steady uphill walk towards the ruined town. I take no notice of the scurrying little beasts that seek to end a night of foraging without becoming prey to an owl or a falcon. As I advance to higher ground, the dark barren hillocks the locals call *calanchi* come into view. Their stark beauty is all too familiar and I ignore them.

At the town's gate, which is boarded to keep intruders away, I run—as I often do—into the shepherd boy who leads his goats, and the mule he calls Clarissa, crosstown toward the pastures to the west. He cannot be older than nine and has the striking, mixed-race looks of the natives of Basilicata. He bends his head respectfully (perhaps fearfully) and mutters a greeting or a prayer I do not hear. I wave at him and move on.

I cross the overgrown streets of the ancient town, avoiding the debris that covers the ground, always going uphill. I pass structures fallen into ruin; decrepit palaces and churches still showing remnants of the shutters, railings and frescoes that once graced them. At last, I arrive at the chosen meeting place. Rosalba awaits me, standing by a stone slab that serves as a bench, at the entrance of the highest structure in the city: the long-abandoned Norman Tower. She is pale, but her features remain as beautiful as ever.

"You are late," she complains, in a voice laden with recrimination.

"I am not," I reply flatly and sit next to her.

I try to hold her hand but, as always, Rosalba shies from my touch. "What do you have to say for yourself?" she asks with asperity.

"Nothing much," I reply. "I spend most of the time thinking about you, about us, about the life we used to have."

"Bah!" replies Rosalba dismissively. "Even in the best of times, our life was nothing to brag about. You worked the fields, I cared for our home, we went together to Sunday Mass and to the festival of Saint Vincenzo in October. One boring season after another, year after year."

"But there was always love."

"Perhaps at first. Then your jealousy destroyed all we had."

"There was a reason for jealousy. Can you deny that the town men made eyes at you, that you returned their glances and flirted with them?"

"Well, a woman always likes to be admired. It was not my fault to be pretty. But in my heart, I was always faithful to you."

"Always?"

"Always."

"How can you say that? You know it is not true. I caught you right here in the arms of Tulio, that filthy baker from Potenza."

"Tulio meant nothing to me. Only a passing fancy, though there was more than that on his part. He was handsome and virile and treated me with respect. Every day he would bake a wonderful loaf of Pane di Matera for us and bring it over to our hut, as a gift."

"And you sold yourself to him for a loaf of bread!" The fury that never goes away fills my mouth with bile.

"Not so. I felt I owed him a few kisses in exchange for his kindness. We came to this abandoned tower to be away from the town gossips. I never lay with him, never touched him, before you caught us—"

"I can't believe you still claim you were faithful to me! Putana!" I rise from the stone slab and wave a menacing fist at her.

Rosalba utters a thin laugh. "You can't hurt me any more than you did."

"I did what I had to do," I groan.

"You found us together in this tower, and murdered us both."

"I had been following you, and by the time I got here I was too angry to control my actions."

"You knifed Tulio twice on the chest and that was that for him. He was almost peaceful as he died in my arms. But what you did to me…"

"Please, stop!" I beg.

Rosalba goes on, implacable. "You butchered me, and buried me while I was still not quite dead!" Her voice rises in a dark torrent.

"Please, stop!" I beg again, in vain.

"You dug a hole in the dirt and dumped me there. That mound marks the spot."

"I know..." I whimper.

"I lie there, on the cold earth, without a Christian burial, without a hearse, food for the wolves and the maggots, like a dead animal."

"I had to bury you. I feared I would be charged with murdering you if your body was discovered."

"At least you dragged Tulio's body away and dropped it on the main road, where he would be found. He rests in peace. But I..."

"I would love to remove you from the earth and give your remains a proper burial, if I only could..."

"You cannot, and I forbid it."

"But then, please, release me from these encounters!" I beg. "I cannot endure the torment."

"Yet you feel no remorse for your actions. You still think your murders were justified. You regret nothing!"

"It's too late for regrets," I cry.

Our bickering continues, in endless repetition, through the day and into the late afternoon. As the sun starts setting, Rosalba says with finality: "You are beyond redemption. So, I will never release you. I command you to return tomorrow. Don't be late."

Rosalba's figure becomes immaterial, translucent, almost invisible as it sinks to the earth beneath the little mound. I remain sitting on the stone slab, watching without seeing how my long-dead wife disappears for another day. A cloud drifts across from the late afternoon sky and everything is suddenly engulfed in darkness. A gust of the wind that always blows on this hill elicits groans and creaks from the deserted houses below.

I have lingered too long in my daily dispute with Rosalba's ghost: the last strands of pink sunset light fade from the tops of the calanchi. I get up slowly and go inside the building. Finding my way by touching the walls, I ascend a long set of stone steps that take me to the square roof of the tower. There I remain for a long time, watching as night creeps over the countryside. It had been painful for me to watch from this vantage point when the townspeople had to move away because the landslides and quakes made it unsafe for them to remain.

The view of the deserted town below, cast in shadows in the fading twilight, envelopes me like a shroud of melancholy. What is left for me? All that I once loved was gone, taken away by my own hand. I should go away forever, as the townspeople did.

I climb onto the parapet that encircles the top of the tower, and balance myself against the rising evening wind. Should I do it? Why not? What is there to linger on for?

As I crouch to gather momentum for the fatal plunge to the cobblestones below, I have a strange sense of familiarity, as if the muscles of my thighs are readying for a practiced exercise. I take a deep breath and leap.

Midway through the air, though, I remember—as I do every night at this moment—that the release I seek is forever being denied me. Like many previous jumps, this one cannot possibly kill me. The first one, years ago, already did.

MATIAS TRAVIESO-DIAZ is an engineer and attorney, born in Cuba and retired after half a century of professional practice. Following retirement, he has taken up creative writing and authored many short stories of various lengths and genres. Over forty of his stories have appeared or are scheduled to appear in paying short story anthologies, magazines, audio books and podcasts.

EVERYTHING
SHE'S LOOKING FOR

Caitlin Marceau

"I think I want to break up with you."

"Oh my God, shut up," she laughs. "I said I was sorry."

"No, I mean it," the other woman jokes, "I think we need to break up. I was promised a night of—how did the e-vite phrase it?— 'furiously feminist and devilishly divine fun.' That, Morgan, was fucking lame."

The leaves crunch underfoot as they walk through the dimly lit park, putting distance between themselves and the small university-owned townhouse a few streets over. The air is cool on their skin and promises rain. Wind rushes through the trees and rattles the branches, shaking out the last of the autumn-red foliage onto the ground ahead of them. The stars are bright overhead, or they would be if not for the glowing city lights drowning out their natural beauty.

"I didn't know you were into that Wicca shit," Ari says, with a smile.

"I'm not! Or like, not like whatever the hell that was."

"Sure, whatever you say. Next thing I know you'll be BFFs with Raven Blackfeather Ceridwen and her troupe of radical truth-seeking sisters of the moon."

Morgan laughs, nearly doubling over. "*Man*, was she pretentious or what?"

"I mean, what else were you expecting from a university Wiccan group?"

"Can you say their title properly, please? They were *very* clear about how they identified their organisation."

"Right, sorry. What did you expect from a university-funded interfaith coven for socially conscious babes made of starlight?"

The two of them laugh with abandon before Morgan thinks to make sure none of the other meeting members are within earshot. Thankfully, they are alone in the park as they head to the student housing district a few blocks over. With cheap rent, cheap amenities (like the park), and cheap bars within walking distance of nearly all the downtown campus buildings, Laughlan Street East is known primarily for housing most of the city's university students. With a variety of apartment buildings practically stacked on top of each other for a three-block radius, most of the students are—to some varying degree—both neighbours and classmates. Morgan and Ari are no exception, having found themselves in the same Research Methods class and apartment complex.

"I don't know. I mean, I guess something more... *more*. Like, I guess I was expecting them to do small spells and rituals, maybe. And like, get more involved with protests and social justice work. Not sit in a living room and act pretentious while drowning in a sea of palo santo."

"Yeah, that was a lot."

"So strong," Morgan agrees. "The smell was the most powerful thing about that group."

"I'll take it you're not planning on joining them for next month's Goddess Circle?"

"I'd sooner choke."

The two of them walk in silence for a bit, the noise of the downtown core filtering through the trees. The park, although small, is a green shelter from the all-consuming sea of grey brick around them. The maples offer shade on hot days and something sturdy to make out against at night, and even without most of their leaves, they dull the noise of drunk students and honking cars. Their building, the tallest one on the rapidly approaching block, is obscured from view thanks to a collection of lush pines in the distance.

"So, what made you want to go tonight? Spirituality? New friends?" Ari asks in earnest.

"Oh, it doesn't matter. It's stupid."

"I doubt it. Come on, you can tell me."

Morgan exhales and looks away, embarrassed, though not for the first time that evening. "The magic." Ari laughs and Morgan crosses her arms in front of her chest defensively. "I told you it was stupid."

"Oh, no, sorry! I wasn't laughing at you, I promise. And that's not stupid."

"I feel pretty stupid."

"No, don't! Really, don't. You're not stupid, you're wonderful." She paws at Morgan's arms, uncrossing them and taking her hands in Ari's own, pulling her closer. "I was laughing that you went to a bunch of Wiccans for a taste of magic when I'm right here."

"You are *so* lame when you're trying to be romantic," Morgan laughs, leaning in and kissing Ari on the lips. "Thankfully, you're cute."

"First of all, I'm gorgeous," she teases. "And secondly, I wasn't trying to be romantic, I was being serious."

They continue through the park, out to the main street, and then cross at the intersection to their building. They open the main glass door, punch the door code into the second one, and get in the small elevator together. The two of them get off on the sixth floor and Ari walks Morgan to her door.

"Well, tonight was… interesting," Ari laughs, as Morgan unlocks her apartment.

"You could say that."

Ari chuckles and leans in, planting a soft kiss on Morgan's cheek. "Have I mentioned how beautiful you look tonight? You're fucking radiant."

Morgan smiles and looks down. "*You're* radiant. I'm… I just wish…"

"What?"

"I wish I could be more like you."

"Now, why would you want to do a silly thing like that?"

Morgan ducks the question and asks one of her own instead. "See you tomorrow in class?"

"Definitely."

Ari brushes a lock of Morgan's hair behind her ear, and when she pulls back her hand she's holding a single peony between her fingers. She hands it to the other woman with a smile and heads back down the hall to the elevator.

"How'd you do that?"

Ari waves without looking back.

She taps her nails along the side of the coffee cup, the trimmed ovals clicking against the thick cardboard impatiently as she waits. She picks up the peony again, running her fingers over the stem, across the leaves, and between each petal as she admires the flower.

"Hey!" Ari calls from the doorway of the coffee shop, crossing through the crowded room. She leans down and kisses her before taking a seat across from Morgan at the small round table.

"Hey! I got this for you," she says, sliding one of the disposable cups across the marbled surface. "It's not the pumpkin one, before you ask."

"Thank fuck," she says with a smile, gulping the hot caffeine.

"More for me."

"And I hope you enjoy every sip of it," she says, wrinkling her nose as her girlfriend takes a gulp. "You liked the flower I gave you enough to drag it around all day?"

"I'm honestly just trying to figure out how you did it."

"With magic."

"Haha."

Ari tilts her head to one side, raising an eyebrow. "I'm not joking. It's witchcraft. Magic with a capital 'M.' Spellcasting. Whatever you want to call it, that thing you were looking for with the coven last night, that's what I used to make you a flower."

"Come on, stop messing with me."

Ari frowns and pulls the pink peony across the table towards her. She covers the petals with her hands and closes her eyes. After an uncomfortably long moment, she opens them, smiles at Morgan, and lifts her hands to reveal the now black petals. Morgan stares at her, eyebrow raised. Ari covers it once more and closes her eyes. This time, when she reveals the flower, it's a yellow rose. As if to out-do herself, she repeats the process a third a final time, leaving a violet and white lisianthus in her wake.

Morgan stares at the flower for a long time before reaching out to touch it. She moves slow, like she's worried the plant might bite her, and picks it up delicately. She turns the flower between her fingers before staring at Ari.

"Wow. Just... wow," Morgan breathes, "that's... wow."

"Wow?"

"I mean, what can I even say?"

"Showering me with praise for my awe-inspiring power is always a good place to start," Ari jokes.

"I am in awe over your power," Morgan says, quietly.

The other woman frowns and folds her hands in her lap. "Seriously, though, are you okay? Have I freaked you out with this? You seem, I don't know, shellshocked about this. About magic."

"Magic isn't real."

"I thought it's what you were looking for at the coven yesterday?"

"Yeah, I mean, I was," Morgan stammers, "but like? I don't know? I didn't *really* expect to find it. Not really."

"Didn't you, though?" Ari pushes. "Because you seemed pretty let down when you went home."

"I mean, I guess I was a little hopeful."

"So you *were* looking for magic then."

"Hoping and actively looking are two different things."

"Hoping is like the lazy man's version of looking. It's searching for something greater than one's self and assuming you'll come up empty-handed, but that *maybe* you'll find something eventually. And, besides, if you're hoping for magic then it means at least a small part of you believes in the possibility of it."

Morgan drinks from her latte as she digests everything. Eventually, she nods, conceding that there's some truth to Ari's words. She picks the lisianthus up again, looking at it from every side, feeling the petals, and running her hand over the stem.

"Why?" Morgan eventually asks.

"Why what?"

"Why are you showing me this? Why are you showing me magic? Does this make you a witch? Are you going to have to kill me or wipe my memory clean? What does this mean for me?"

"Wow, okay, a bit of a floodgate, but I'm into it," Ari jokes. She reaches across the table and takes Morgan's hands in her own, holding them gently. "Yes, I'm a witch. And, not to freak you out, but I think you might be one too. I could feel this, energy? Power? *Something* in you when we first met. And it's not the reason I fell in—well—fell for you. I actually thought you knew you had magic, but then you never brought it up, and there was the Wicca date, and I realised pretty quickly you didn't know."

"You think I'm powerful?"

"Fuck yes. *And* I think you might have magic, so bonus," she teases. "So, for your other big questions, I'm showing you magic because if you're a witch then you should learn how to use the gifts you've been given, and know that you don't have to go looking for divinity in other people when you have it inside of you. And if you're not a witch, then I still really like you. Like, a lot. I think I might even," she exhales and gives Morgan a sad smile. "Anyways, I guess I just wanted to share this with you because you're special. And now I kinda hope I haven't freaked you out too much and scared you away forever," she says nervously.

"No! Definitely not," Morgan rushes, squeezing Ari's hand back. "I mean, yeah, it's a lot to take in, but you haven't scared me with anything. And I like you too. A lot."

"Really?"

"Yeah, definitely. And, you know, if you're ever comfortable with it, I'd love to see more of what you can do."

"Come on then," Ari says excitedly, standing up from her chair and pulling Morgan to her feet.

"Where are we going?"

"To make magic."

"You're *so* lame," Morgan chuckles, letting the other woman lead the way back to the apartment complex, the lisianthus left discarded on the table.

The inside of Morgan's apartment is warm and comfortable. A pot of tea sits on the kitchen counter, Earl Grey steeping inside. On the small living room coffee table a few candles have been arranged and lit, sage incense burning in a nearby dish. The two women stand with their backs to the mustard sofa, eyes glued to the painting hanging on the wall across from it.

"So, it's going to be hard to access your magic at first," Ari explains, her chin resting on Morgan's shoulder as she stands behind her. "It'll get easier over time and with practice, I promise, but for now it's going to feel like you're trying to reach through a brick wall."

"Sounds fun."

"And yet decidedly not. Lucky for you, I'm going to lend you some of my magic."

"You can do that?"

"Only to other witches, and only if I let you into my heart."

"What do you mean?"

"You'll see," Ari assures her. "For now, just look at the painting on the wall and imagine something *else* was painted on the canvas instead. Think in as much detail as you can. The more specific you can get, the better the results. Once you know what you want, close your eyes and focus your intentions on the canvas."

"Uh, okay," she says hesitantly.

"Don't worry, you're going to suck. Everyone does the first time."

"That's encouraging."

"I'm nothing if not motivational," Ari coos into her ear, "but this is just for practice. I'm more interested in *if* you can cast a spell than if it turns out good."

"Okay."

"You ready?"

"Yeah."

"Okay, I'm letting you in. You should feel it in a second, and once you do, focus on the painting."

It doesn't take long for Morgan to feel Ari's energy, and soon her body is flooded with warmth. No, with *emotion*. It's strong and overwhelming, and feels white-hot coursing through her veins and into her heart. It's love and acceptance and *home*. It makes her feel giddy and alive, and she doesn't want the feeling to end. Never again. She can hear Ari whispering in her ear about the painting, and it takes her a moment to focus on what she's supposed to be doing. Eventually, her mind quiets long enough for Morgan to picture a pink galaxy, swirling and effervescent, and she closes her eyes as she pictures every star and beam of light. When she opens her eyes, the colour block painting has been replaced with the rose galaxy that had lived only in her mind a moment ago.

"Wow," Ari breathes behind her, tickling her neck and sending goosebumps running down her spine. "That's… that's fucking incredible." She moves from behind Morgan and crosses the small space between her and the painting. The galaxy is so exact, it could be a photograph. The stars look as though they're expanding into the depths of the ether, the pink gases swirling across the canvas and seemingly off its corners. "I'm serious, Morgan. This is amazing by practiced witch standards, never mind someone's first time. I don't even think *I* could do that."

"Hey, without you it wouldn't have been possible in the first place. It's *because* of you that I was able to realise something this beautiful. Something like you."

Ari smiles at her and closes the distance between them, taking Morgan's face in her hands and drawing her close. As they kiss, Morgan runs her hands through Ari's long hair and to the nape of her neck. She pulls back from the other woman, breathing heavily.

"Did you mean what you said, back at the coffee place?" Morgan asks.

"About?"

"The way you feel about me. Do you really, you know…"

"Love you?"

"Yeah."

"Yeah. I love you."

Morgan's smile is as radiant as the galaxy on the wall. She kisses Ari deep and pulls away from her lips before planting another soft peck on her.

"I thought I could feel that from you, but I wanted to be sure. Can I try one more spell?"

"Sure, of course."

Ari puts her hands on Morgan's shoulders and opens her heart back up to the woman. Morgan's mouth falls open from the high of it as she drinks in the power.

"You need to do something," Ari reminds her, nodding to the photo.

"I already am," Morgan says, regretfully.

Ari raises an eyebrow and watches the canvas, waiting for the photo to change. It doesn't. But something inside her does. At first, it feels like a small pressure building within her, but soon she's doubled over, clutching at her chest as a searing pain runs through her bones.

"Stop, Morgan, stop! Wh-whatever you're trying to do, stop. I-I don't think it's working."

"It is, don't worry."

"No, please, y-you need to—"

"Calm down, Ari. It's almost over. I'm so sorry, baby."

"What i-is? Wh-y are you sorry?"

"Did you know witches don't have an infinite supply of this shit?" Morgan asks her, trying to lead her first to the couch, and then helping Ari onto the ground as her knees give way. "I didn't. Apparently, it's why witches had covens in the first place, so they could borrow and replenish each other's magic. But for solo practitioners? We just, I don't know, *stop*. The magic goes away, the well runs dry, and we just stop having power."

"Wh-what are you talking a-about?" Ari asks, blinking slowly.

Morgan helps Ari lie down on her side before walking over to the couch, grabbing a pillow, and bringing it back to the woman. She lifts Ari's head and slides the pillow underneath it before brushing hair off the woman's forehead with a delicate hand.

"I'm really sorry you had to fall in love with me to make this work, but you said it yourself, you needed to let me into your heart to use your magic. And an open heart, a *vulnerable* heart, makes tapping into power—draining that power—a lot easier. You *are* an amazing woman, though. And you know, in another life, I think we could have worked out."

Morgan opens her mouth trying to say something, but another wave of pain rolls through her and she seizes up from the agony of it.

"I hope, in another universe, that we did work out. That we're happy and growing old together."

"Wh-at a-are you t-talking about?" she slurs, vision blurring at the edges. There's a pit in her stomach that gets bigger with every passing second, but she's too weak to move. Her breathing is slowing down, her limbs heavy.

"I hope you know how beautiful you really are and how much your strength has inspired me. I hope you know that I wish, *I wish*, this could be any other way," Morgan whispers to her, unaware that all Ari can hear is the blood slowing in her veins. "I'm so sorry, Ari. I hope you know, despite all this, I love you too."

She looks down at Ari's still body with a sad smile, holding her until her body feels cold to the touch. Eventually, Morgan leans over and kisses her on the forehead before closing her eyes and focusing her intentions. When she opens them, Ari's body is gone from the living room floor. Morgan gets up and passes the canvas, chest tight as she looks at the kaleidoscopic galaxy.

Ari stares back, portrait arranged in the painted stars.

CAITLIN MARCEAU is an author and professional editor living and working in Montreal. She holds a B.A. in Creative Writing and is a member of the Horror Writers Association. If she's not covered in ink or wading through stacks of paper, you can find her ranting about issues in pop culture or nerding out over a good book. For more visit caitlinmarceau.ca.

THE LOVELIEST CORPSE

Simone le Roux

When I die, I hope they send me into the ocean. I've read that's what the Vikings would do. They'd float someone out onto the fjord surrounded by flowers and jewels and gold and precious creations, then set it all ablaze.

I think I would look quite beautiful that way: my pallid skin made paler by the bright flowers woven into my hair, the gold on my feet and fingers catching the light, a shield across my still breast. In my mind's eye, I'm lit by moonlight even as my boat catches fire, even as I sink, sizzling, into the icy waters below.

I would lie on the ocean floor, weighed down by my charred shield. Miraculously untouched by the flames, my porcelain visage would be preserved in the cold, salty waters. Silver fish would dart among the floating strands of my dark hair. I'd be the most beautiful thing that nobody would ever see.

I often find myself lying in bed and dreaming of being the loveliest corpse at the bottom of a distant fjord. I imagine that the waters feel as my blankets do: a comforting heaviness. I've been in bed for so long I can almost feel the crabs weathering my fingertips, the algae spreading along my arms. My hair tickles my face as it whisps around me in a halo.

Sometimes I imagine someone finding me. He would have lost something precious to him—a ring for his betrothed, perhaps—and jumped from his longship to retrieve it. He would find me instead and, at the disturbance of his presence, my arm would come loose from the sand and float upwards, as though I was reaching for him. He would see my lovely face, my crown of fish and flowers, my gold-tipped feet, and he would fall in love. He would take my ragged hand and join me on the sun-dappled ocean floor, where he would rest forever.

What would it be like, to have spent so long at the bottom of the ocean and at last be joined by someone? To be seen and known and loved? I suppose I shall never know.

Mother's companionship doesn't chase away the loneliness. I know, I'm fortunate to be cared for so well. Poor Mother, who was tired and old even before I became ill, tends to my every need. She sits beside me for hours, even though I must be tedious company. I spend my time drifting in and out of sleep and, in the twilight between, I believe my dreams are real, or I doubt my reality. Once or twice when I awoke, I told Mother we were late to catch my boat! Can you imagine? She had the grace not to laugh at me.

That was the first symptom of my illness, in fact: the doctors suggested it was something akin to early dementia.

The first dream I remember believing was one where I walked the halls of our home in grimy darkness. I know now it must have been a dream because our home has always been exceptionally clean. When

Mother was young, before my uncle squandered the family's fortune, she had servants. She became used to a certain standard and, even as our home fell into disrepair, she tasked me with keeping it spotless. This is the lot of the oldest child, I suppose. I was always more of a colleague than a daughter. As soon as I could walk, she showed me how to keep the house in order and then left me to get on with things.

Where was I? Oh yes, my dream. In the dream, the house looked dreadful. It's always been somewhat gloomy—being next to the sea causes terrible damp and decay—but in the dream it was as if the house hadn't seen my touch for a long time. Cobwebs lined the corners; dust coated the floors and paintings, puffing up as I stepped on the carpets; and dark mould crept along the walls. Even the silver looked tarnished: a cardinal sin in our household. In the dream, I was drawn to a sputtering, strange light from the library. When I peered through the half-closed door, I found the fireplace alight. It must have been filled with driftwood because the flames had a green tinge to them.

Mother knelt, naked, in front of the fire, holding something to her chest that I couldn't quite see. It was undulating in a twitching staccato that matched the rhythm of blood in my own ears. From beside her, Mother picked up a sharp blade that glinted cold green in the light of the fire. She lifted the pulsing thing high above her head and plunged the knife into it. In the dream, I clapped my hand over my mouth to stifle my scream. The thing shuddered, and then slowed to stillness. Blood dribbled out of Mother's cupped hands, down her forearms, and into her waiting mouth.

I was so ill I spent the first week of my fever believing it was real. Mother has been ever so patient and kind to me through all this, even as I accused her of horrific things. And to think, I was an ungrateful daughter before all this.

Growing up, I was an agreeable girl. I think I told you already that I was responsible for keeping the house in order, which was fine with me. Because of the way she grew up, Mother doesn't have the same constitution for hard work that I do—did, I suppose. I loved looking after my little brother and sister as well. They were such darling children, and I didn't wish them to want for anything.

Of course, after my sister got married and my brother passed away, it was hard to find as much purpose in my days. I'm sure Mother felt the same way, having looked after all three of us for many years. I was never a great beauty, and I hadn't had much time for men, so I knew marriage was not an immediate prospect for me. Instead, I got it in my head that I ought to join my cousin in Paris for a few months and perhaps learn some sort of artisanal skill. I had begun to make the arrangements before I became sick.

I realise now what a wild flight of fancy that was, travelling alone and leaving Mother to fend for herself. To learn how to work! What a disgrace for Mother, to be abandoned by her spinster daughter.

I wouldn't say it to Mother, but I think it's doing her good having me to look after. The new purpose seems to have invigorated her. When we eat together, I watch her devour meals that a grown man would find more than filling. With this new appetite, her cheeks are filling out, ironing away the wrinkles that had rested in their hollows.

Her complexion is rosier and, perhaps owing to my failing eyesight, her hair appears to have darkened to the same colour as mine.

She's in good spirits, too, even though it must sadden her dreadfully to see me in such a state. She talks and reads to me even as I'm sleeping, until all the words turn into a dull chant in my tired mind. Sometimes I wish she wouldn't, as I find myself somehow more exhausted than I was before I went to sleep.

My dreams of the ocean floor take on a darker tone when she's with me. I am not a pale sleeping beauty when Mother sits beside me. Rather, I am a blackened skeleton, unadorned and imprisoned on the ocean floor by the weight of my shield in almost total darkness. The luminescent eyes of improbable sea creatures look on and fish swim in and out of my eye sockets. If I had eyes, I would only be able to make out the faint shapes of ships as they pass by above me, oblivious to the gaping thing below.

I can't be expected to heal with visions like that in my head, but I imagine healing isn't a possibility for me anymore.

It at least makes me glad to think that, when I do depart this earth, Mother will be well enough to go on. I don't have much longer here, but Mother shushes me every time I try to discuss it. I suppose I don't have any affairs that need to be put in order. I keep trying to tell her about my dreams of an ocean burial, but she won't hear of it. She intends to put me in the family crypt, where I will be surrounded by stone until the end of days.

"You need to be with your brother and father," she says. "They have been utterly lost without you to care for them, I'm sure."

"Will you be alright, Mother?" I ask her as I feel myself sink into sleep again. "Who will look after you when I'm gone?"

Mother smiles through her fresh, smooth face and I can see light dancing in her once dull eyes. "You've done enough."

SIMONE LE ROUX is a third culture kid still trying to figure out the culture part. As someone who studied neuroscience and a lover of all things spooky, she focuses on what makes our minds the biggest boogiemen of all. The Loveliest Corpse *is Simone's first published piece.*

HOLD YOUR SISTER
UNTIL YOU CAN'T ANYMORE
Cara Mast

We drown Dahla in the canal behind the house. She should be too far gone at this point to fight, but fight she does, with teeth and nails and spirit we haven't seen for months since she started wasting away with the sickness. We are so proud.

We haven't had a River Girl in the family in a very long time.

We waited this long because all three of us sisters have been sick. We got better. Dahla did not. The doctor said it was up to God to save her, but we're afraid to wait on God. What if He wants her more than we do?

So we take her down to the water as soon as we can carry her between the two of us, one of her spindly, ashen arms slung over each of our narrow shoulders. Three girls stealing out from their beds for a breath of fresh air after the stuffy oppression of the sickroom. Fresher air. The canal stinks of rubbish and rot, but the brine beneath cuts off the cloying sweet of sickness and the poor attempts to disguise it. Dahla perks up slightly at the change in atmosphere, and she gets somehow heavier as she brushes up against lucidity. We grunt at the effort of pulling her down to the side of the canal, but we can't help smiling through our tears as she tilts her face toward the sun, sighing without pain. Beyond pain.

Dahla hated dying, back when she still had the sense to understand what was happening to her. We all hated it, but then we pulled back from death's precipice, and Dahla settled down at its crumbling edge. She can't fall over it, we can't let her.

We edge our way into the water at the empty boat slip, the sunken stone steps into the water increasingly slick the deeper we go. At first, Dahla does not seem to notice our feet are wet. But she changes from ghost to beast when we drop her in the water fully. Her howl is not that of a dying thing. It is the ragged tear of a desperate thing. We can't say if her dulled gaze sharpens back to living focus because we both grab a fistful of her lank hair and shove her under the murky surface of the water.

She thrashes, fighting to get out from under our grip, back up to the air. We have enough sense to grab the railings nearest us with our free hands. If she wasn't so weakened by the sickness, she might have dragged us out into the depths of the canal with her. Dahla flails, kicking at our feet, hitting at our bodies. Scratching our legs, bare in the water as our nightgowns float around our waists. We fear in her rage she might bash her own head against the stone stairs, and so we hold her steady even as we keep her under; we don't know much about how to make a River Girl, but it won't work if she's all broken up, because what use is a broken River Girl?

The water is cold, and it gets harder for us to keep our grips, on the railings and on our sister. She has an advantage here, since her fight is all reflex, and our perseverance is effort. It would be easy to let her go. But then she would end up just another corpse, another body for the fires. And that is more unbearable to us than drowning our sister and turning her into something that is not our sister, but also not dead. If God wanted a say, He should have healed her like He did us.

We mutter the spell through chattering teeth as we curl our cold-warped hands tighter in Dahla's hair. Her body jerks, shudders. Bubbles rush around the sides of her head in a burst. She stills, finally, her hands falling limp against our feet. We raise our voices, hesitant at first and then louder in our hurried panic to get it right. We have to flip her over. Her face is a mask that no longer resembles our sister. Skin, loosened as fever melted the last pockets of fat off her cheeks, has swollen with the water forced inside her. We pull her slack jawed mouth open wider. Shove the wooden token and the clips of our hair and the jagged grey scale to the back of her tongue and press her mouth closed. Cry out the final words of the spell.

How do we make a dead girl swallow? we think nervously as we hold Dahla's mouth closed and wait. Dead girls can't swallow.

Dahla's body slides down into the canal. We grab for her in horror, but our hands are batted away. Her skin doesn't feel like skin. Her hands don't feel like hands. We shiver on the canal steps, searching through the dark water for any sign of our sister, her white nightgown, anything.

The dress surfaces first, but we shriek at the sharp and strong teeth biting our submerged ankles. We scramble out of the water, matching crescents bleeding on our legs. We stare at the nightgown as it's pushed toward shore ahead of a waterlogged head of hair. The head rises out of the water, and it's Dahla but not. Her wide forehead and pointed chin remain, but the skin over that face has deepened its grey to that of an oily smoke, and the eyes set in the grey face are too large and too wet even if they still hold the warm brown of Dahla's eyes.

The River Girl sinks down again until only her eyes are above the water. She waits. Watches. Until we reach out and pull Dahla's abandoned nightgown onto the dry stone of the wall above the canal. The River Girl blinks her big eyes, spits canal water at us, and then dives into the middle of the canal.

Later, when Ma and Da ask us where Dahla is, we burst into tears as we explain, "She went down to the water!"

We hold her sodden nightgown between us, and when Da tries to take it from us, we wail all the louder and clutch it tight. Clutch each other tight. He cannot have the last thing she gave us, but of course we can't tell him that.

We don't see the River Girl again. She lets us know she visits, though.

A necklace Ma loses over the side of our boat on the way to church one morning shows up at the canal-side door of our house a week later. Our cat, Kippy, who is free to wander the alleys and canal walks, disappears for a few days and returns soaking wet with some of his fur rubbed off. He does not leave the house after his return, ever again.

He does not let us pet him again, either. Da's boat stops leaking, and rides steadier than it used to. When someone tries to steal Da's boat at the market, they fall into the canal, and no one can remember seeing them after.

We put crowns made of flowers, almond candies, and little folded notes in baskets that we float off the back of our house at each of Dahla's birthdays. The baskets always come back, empty except for a grey scale or two wedged into the basket's weave.

We split the scales between us, and wear them in small pouches around our necks. The River Girl keeps coming back, mostly as a blessing. We thank God for her, and wonder if this wasn't His plan all along.

As a retired tall-ship sailor, a failed academic, and a millennial finance professional, CARA MAST is someone who gets stopped constantly in New York City and asked for directions. Cara spends their free time drinking coffee, binging words, and yelling about the Philadelphia Eagles in their apartment and family group chat. They can be found on Twitter @digicara, and at digicara.com.

THE BLOOM

Jenna Junior

I don't know how it started to appeal to me, but I do know why I stayed. My husband and I had joined the group together. Our marriage was perfect from the outside and seemed perfect on the inside. Our parents had been friends in college. We played together as children. All my life, I was told this is how it should be. Love was something that could be grown, my mother often whispered to me.

On our wedding night and the years we had spent together after, I worked hard on trying to grow our love. I believe I did a decent job. I would bring him his morning paper. I would clean the house as he napped on Sunday afternoons. At night, I would touch him and he would touch me, and I believed that it was enough. I convinced myself that it was something I enjoyed.

However, even when things seemed completely idyllic, I was always looking for something. I don't know if he felt the same and frankly, I never cared to ask. I felt the kind of feeling you get when you lose a puzzle piece and it's the only thing left to complete the full picture. No matter where I went or what we did, I couldn't find that piece. Then we met the Organizer, and the piece was right there in front of me.

We joined because we wanted to fill a void, one we couldn't name. What filled that void was her.

I know people expect there to be a reason for going along with this. I think that may actually be the problem in itself... the search for a reason. One clue leads to another, and you're following bread crumbs until you don't remember where you started from. All you know is that you're deep in the woods, and, after a time, you become lost. That's how I felt when I joined them. I felt like I had been searching for something for so long. Maybe I was just wanting to rest at last, or maybe I felt I had truly found the answer to all my questions. I'm not sure anymore. These things now feel abstract.

I didn't even know I was the way I am until I saw her. She had the face I always imagined bakers to have—rosy, apple cheeked, soft. They call her "fat" and "sloppy" in the papers and wonder why anyone would want to hear what a woman like her has to say. I don't think those people have ever craved warmth like I have. In her face, I saw a mother figure. Not my own mother, who would throw away the puzzles I worked on at the tiny table in my bedroom because they "dirtied" a space that was supposedly my own. The Organizer was a mother of fairy tales, who would know something was wrong just with a glance. She could do this not just with me, but with everyone in the commune.

She was also a mother in the sense that I was constantly seeking her approval while being hyper-aware I had the ability to disappoint her. She was maternal like the earth, soft and giving at times, yet stubborn when conditions were not right. Still, I finally saw a place where my love could grow, and even more, a place where it could bloom. I saw a blanket fort where no one could find me. I saw a clearing in the woods where mushrooms on fallen logs gleamed in the sun, like butter pads melting onto warm bread. I saw home, and not just as a physical place, but also as a virtue. She was everything I had ever wanted and never believed I could have.

When she spoke, her eyes would dwell on you so you knew she could hear you, even if she was the one talking. She could touch you with a look, her eyes lighting on you like a reassuring hand. She wasn't just soft, though. She was powerful. She wore her body like she knew what it was for. I imagined it curling around me in the dark, my lanky frame being swallowed by hers, a puzzle piece connecting with a satisfying, exhilarating *click*. I had no idea if she would accept me, a woman, into her bed and her heart.

Back in the time before, now a memory growing hazier every day, I had only heard harsh whispers for women with feelings like me. I had heard those whispers and thought that perhaps the gossip was intertwined with a truth I had not discovered. Perhaps there was something sinister lurking beneath women's longing. Now, I realise, it was jealousy formed out of a desperate wish to feel the same. Once touched by such a passion, I believe one could find herself chasing it until it destroyed her completely.

I had seen her reject men in the community who were attracted to her, but I have also always found men to be counterproductive to the schemes of women. She was cunning, and I knew her ambitions laid beyond those of normal, ordinary people. To the other members, she was righteous. She quoted the Bible easily, with the ease of clergy we all had experienced our entire lives. When her rituals became more peculiar—the word I see in countless articles—it was easy to fool these people into thinking they were still in something familiar. I, however, saw her ambition like a weapon and instead of fearing it, it exhilarated me.

When I was a young girl, my father let me hold a gun he had used in the war. My father and I were close in a quiet way, where neither one of us would express affection verbally because it was something understood. I have heard on the radio, men speculating that something was wrong with my home life to make me do the things I did. I admit, I was never truly happy, but until I met the Organizer, it was just something missing from my understanding. Still, there was nothing *wrong*. My father loved me and my mother tolerated me and for a very long time, that was all I could ever ask for because I had not learned I could ask for more.

When my father let me hold his gun, an Enfield rifle with a stain near the trigger I never inquired about, I did not feel fear. I felt something exciting twist in my stomach, a nervous tingling that hummed from the base of my spine to the tips of my fingers. When I watched the Organizer write tracts in the fading light from the moon, her brow furrowed and her teeth biting deep into her bottom lip, I felt the same nervous delight wind inside of me. When she pressed her warm hands against the fevered foreheads of her followers, sending them down to the ground to grind into the dirt with spiritual ecstasy, I saw the danger in her. She was a weapon that I wanted to hold.

Every time I completed a task, she would congratulate me, but her eyes remained guarded. It was never enough for her. I always had something else to do, and I would do it gladly so I could possibly hear another praise leave her honey lips and maybe, in her eyes, I would see my own reflection as something valuable.

The tasks I would do for her started as things without much consequence. It started with leading prayer circles, something I did with as much zeal as I could muster. I got rather good at it, through the trick of replacing the god I prayed to with her image. That, it turned out, was a wise way of operating, since she slowly transitioned the flock to focus on her own spiritual prowess. Since I was already adept at worshipping her—the way she laughed when she was surprised, the way she loved stray dogs, the smell of her hair when she walked by—I quickly moved up in rank.

This then required me to keep an eye on fellow members. I would eavesdrop, my unassuming stature working in my favour, and report back to her about any dissent. Over time, those dissenters started to vanish. I think my lack of questioning where they went spoke to her. I think the way I was able to clean them up spoke to her, as well.

However, her desire for power grew over time. The more dissent, the more invigorated she became. When members stole off in the night, she started to take it personally. Ultimate control was something she wanted, and, in a way, I can still understand. When you know you're special, why wouldn't you want people to notice you? She wanted more, and this, in turn, made me want her more.

Worship was just an extension of her being. She told us it would bring us enlightenment and ascension. I personally couldn't care less. I just wanted to be in the same world as she was. I have heard people comment that our services were strange, but I never had a moment to examine the practices closely. I was always racing to get closer to her, doing whatever I could with my money, my body, my time, to make her realise how good it would be to have me near.

She acted in a way that made me believe I was *so close* to joining her. Others had seemed more advanced than I, at times, but she would find faults with them and tell them they were not ready for divine understanding. I never wanted that understanding. I wanted her attention, fully, her mouth on mine, knowing every part of her belonged with every part of me. So when she told us what we had to do, I saw my chance.

My husband was always a coward, and this is probably why he married me. I was not an ideal partner. I was cold and callous, I know, and it only got worse when we moved permanently to the camp. Before, my life with him was merely a ritual. It consisted of tiny little acts I had hoped could be viewed as love. When we came to the commune, I was clearly in love with the Organizer, and for a long while—years, in fact. He just chose to believe that meant I was devout.

The things I did for her were more than small acts; I performed every motion with absolute intent. I believe, now, that is what love truly is. It is worship, a devotion that can easily be seen as foolish to those not directly involved. When the Organizer told us what we were to do—that last step in achieving complete awareness—my husband acted in self-preservation. He left the group. He didn't ask me to join him. He just stole away in the night, and I haven't heard anything from or about him since. All I know is I woke up alone, his side of our pallet cold. I was relieved. Now I could join her completely. Now the love I had worked to grow could finally bloom.

I think the only foolish thing I've done was to believe that something would change after we killed them. I did not flinch as I stabbed the woman. Her cries muffled the moment they struck my ears. I did not cringe when I took the children to the edge of the pond. Before, I was told I could tell them it was a kind of game, to make it easier on my mind and theirs. I told them nothing.

I did not blink when the grandmother begged me to spare her. She was like a doll, when I carried her body to the flames. Her blood flowed down my hands, but I only noticed it when I showered in their bathroom. I used their soap, the same bar that had lovingly cleaned all their living bodies, and I could only think of what she would say when I came home. But when I returned, the Organizer merely nodded at me. The sweet reunion I had played often in my mind never came. She was occupied talking to another woman, and her eyes, which had drawn me in like a tide to the moon, were drawing in someone else.

I turned myself in, not because I felt guilt. That's an emotion I'm still waiting for, waiting for it to come alive inside of me when I least expect it. I turned myself in because it was the only way I knew how to hurt her. I told them where to find her. I made them a map that would lead to her bed, the one I often envisioned myself in. I told them what she did, with whom she surrounded herself, how she operated.

All the little things I carried in my heart about her—I turned them inside out, sharpened each like a knife to destroy her.

So, yes, I am nervous here in this courtroom, because I can see her there. I can see *you* there. I used to feel nervous in a way that reminded me I was alive. The kind of nervous you hear on the radio, when men croon on and on about their baby. Now, it is a constant biting. A gnawing at the edges of my ribs and at the centre of my heart.

I know people expect me to feel remorse, and I do. I feel remorse that my love was never enough. I feel remorse that I have let it grow like a weed over my mind just to watch it all rot away. I hope you feel remorse, too. I hope you see me here, not as some desperate apostate, but as the missing piece you never found. I hope you carry that kind of remorse in your belly and that it eats you alive, from the inside out, just as you have done to me.

JENNA JUNIOR lives in Oklahoma with her partner and cats. She has been published in Voices of the Heartland Volume II, The Tulsa Voice *and* The Tulsa Review. *She works as a college writing consultant and is the host of the horror podcast,* Scream Service. *You can contact her by looking into a mirror and saying her name thrice.*

SiSTER SMOKE

Emma Kathryn

I didn't think I'd be back here. At least not for anything other than the occasional family event. I certainly didn't think my sister would be ferrying moving boxes back to my mum's house with me.

The sign that looms over us as my sister crosses the boundary into our home town reads "Welcome to the town of Blaneswater." A smaller sign hangs under it, aged and rusting, that says "Scotland in bloom: town of 2011." Someone has spray painted over it: "Sister Smoke waitz 4 U."

Sure enough, the moment we pass the sign, the smoke descends. A thin layer of grey coats everything. Flakes of ash hit the windscreen from time to time.

Nothing has changed. Nothing at all.

My pregnant sister, Anna, keeps glancing at me with worry as she drives. We haven't spoken for a few miles now. Her worry is making me worry now. I don't want to put her blood pressure up. I should really break the silence. Even if I'm just talking crap.

"Sometimes I forget that this place does this," I say, staring out the window at the drifting smoke. "Or maybe I've just tried to forget it."

"Can't ignore it when you're stuck here," Anna snorts, not bothering with her windscreen wipers. They wouldn't do any good. The ash isn't real, and it evaporates as soon as it hits the glass, anyway. "Hasn't happened in a few months, though. And it was clear when I left this morning."

"Weird," I shrug. "Does she still go for walks?"

"Every time the smoke starts. That's basically the sign that she's awake." Anna glances at me with a brief moment of disbelief. "Can't believe you never noticed that when we were kids."

"I didn't see her every time," I argue. "Maybe because we were scared of her. I tried not to look for her."

Anna snorts again. "That's because you were always inside on the computer."

"True." I nod but keep my forehead pressed against the passenger window.

"We lived right opposite her. I don't know how you missed her. I hated that house," she says with a shiver.

I keep my eyes on the street. A few people walk hurriedly through the smoke. A woman drags a kid and her shopping bags quickly towards a car. Two boys fly by on bikes, desperate to get home. The smoke gets thicker as we get closer to Mum's house. In this part of town, there's nobody on the street.

As Anna pulls up outside Mum's house, the town's only notable landmark sits across the road from our old family home. It's the smouldering ruins of what used to be a big, beautiful home on the corner of the main street and the street we grew up on. Floating outside the wreckage is a white shape with blackened limbs. Fingers curl and twitch and toes barely touch the pavement. A sheet hangs over her burnt form, but there's a shadow of a face there. I don't look any closer.

Sister Smoke is watching us.

"Jesus Christ," I mutter as we climb out of the car. Anna hits a button and the boot of the car springs open. Both the boot and the back seat are stacked high with boxes and suitcases.

"Hey, maybe she just wanted to welcome you home," she says with a grim smirk. My sister cradles her baby bump. "You know I can't help with these boxes, right?"

"Who do you think put them in the car in the first place?" I grumble as I grab the light stuff—the suitcases filled with clothes—first.

The front door opens to reveal my mother, red-eyed and clearly fresh from another crying session. She gives Anna a hug first. It's always Anna first. I love her, but she's literally always been the favourite. And next is me, while I'm still dragging two suitcases behind me.

"My poor baby," Mum croons as she strokes my unwashed hair. I can practically hear her thinking, "What a mess she is." She lets go and holds me at arm's length, taking me in. "He's an idiot, sweetheart. Give him a few days and he'll be right back."

"Thank you for your misplaced optimism, Mum," I say, and I can see Anna pulling a face at Mum from behind her back.

At the very least, Mum takes a box from the back of the car (the one labelled "blankets and bedding", typically, and certainly not any of the ones labelled "books") and ushers me inside.

Sister Smoke stays on the pavement outside the husk of what was once her home and watches as we empty the car of boxes. By the time I get the last box, she's gone.

Mum cleared out what used to be my old room, to the front of the house, facing out onto the street. In spite of her ability to cry at the drop of a hat, my mum has never been a sentimentalist, so Anna's and my old rooms were turned into something more useful. Our family didn't do shrines to their children. Instead, my old room was swiftly turned into Dad's office. After he died, it became Mum's craft room.

Anna's room was turned into the grandkids' space. A playroom with beds for when they stay over. Granted, up until now there was only ever one. Little Tiffany. Now Tiffany has a new baby brother on the way—someone she'll have to share the playroom with. It's at the back of the house so that there is never a chance that the little ones will accidentally catch sight of Sister Smoke through the window.

My new old room is now filled with boxes and half-unpacked suitcases. Mum cleared me some drawers in a dresser and somehow managed to empty a cupboard for me. I spend the evening packing, telling myself this is only temporary.

If I made it out of Blaneswater before, I can do it again.

*

Anna doesn't stay for dinner. She claims she needs to get back home for Tiffany, but we all know that it's really because her husband, Steven, is useless and won't even start cooking without her in the house. I hug my sister and give her baby bump an awkward pat while Mum beams at us both.

"My girls are both back home," she gushes. "I never thought I'd see the day."

Anna rolls her eyes and leaves. Mum and I retreat to the kitchen and I peel potatoes while she cooks chicken. She's babbling away while I try my best not to cry into the sink.

Mum has decked the dining table out like it's Christmas day, which is literally the only time that Dad would sit at it. The rest of the time, he would take his dinner on a tray, sitting in his chair, watching the football. And he certainly wouldn't make dinnertime small talk.

But Mum doesn't stop talking. We eat chicken and potatoes and veg while she tells me about her sewing classes and the girls at the library and something darling Tiffany said last week. She's trying far too hard, but it's kind of nice. She never once mentions Karl.

Mum even brings out a cake she's made for dessert. I really don't feel like me having to move back home at the age of twenty-seven is something worth baking a cake over, but here we are.

We watch something crappy on Netflix and I pretend to laugh for Mum's sake. Every now and then, she gives me those same worried glances that Anna gave me. I don't say anything and act like everything's fine.

*

I get ready for bed and Mum keeps checking on me, asking if I need anything or if the bed's okay. I'm on a pull-out sofa. She wanted to buy a new bed, but I insisted I wouldn't be here long enough to warrant her buying a whole new bed. I hope I'm not here that long, anyway.

Once she's finally accepted that I can suitably settle in the room I spent nineteen years of my life in, she leaves me alone. I close the door and look around. I really did think I'd escaped these walls and here I am, back where I started.

I sigh and settle into bed. The weight of today rests on my chest and I try hard not to cry. Tears prick at the back of my eyes and I press the sleeves of my pyjamas against them as if it'll stop the tears going any further than my eyelids. I fail and start to weep.

I cry for my failed relationship and my failed life and my failed attempt at leaving this hellhole.

Stupidly, I send Karl messages that will never get a reply.

Once I've calmed down a bit, I realise the blinds are still up and the light from the streetlight falls directly onto my pillow. With a deep sigh, I get up and cross the room to close them.

Glancing out the window, I notice that the smoke is back. It's much thicker now that it's night-time. Across the street, the streetlight outside the burnt-out house is out. This is the first time that I've actually noticed that it's crooked and the broken lamp leans in towards the vacant lot.

On the edge of the grass, under the bent lamp, stands Sister Smoke, staring up at my window. Her charred hand twitches, and she slowly reaches up. In what takes an eternity of jerks and convulsions, she points her blacked finger at me. My heart is fit to burst and I rapidly pull the blinds down, blocking out the smoke and the sight of the spectre.

Rushing back to bed, I retreat into my ten-year-old self, pulling the covers over my head and keeping the closed window to my back. Sweat covers my face and runs down my neck. Eventually my heart slows, and I try to convince myself that I survived nineteen years here without her ever hurting me before. Adult rationalisation takes over and I try to sleep. I can't, and I can't decide what keeps me awake more. Sister Smoke or my unanswered messages.

I thought I was through with this.

After a week, I've officially unpacked, but I'm still claiming that this is only for a month or so. In spite of this, I still haven't decided what comes at the end of that self-appointed deadline. Do I move back home? Do I find a new home? Do I curl up in on myself until I simply stop existing?

I'm still not sure.

Anna has appeared with Tiffany, and Mum has baked again. Lemon drizzle cake this time. Apparently, it's Tiffany's favourite. Tiffany is probably the most articulate seven-year-old I've ever met. As she tells us all about school and about the Roald Dahl books she's been devouring lately, I can't help but smile at Anna.

My amazing sister has taken motherhood in her stride. Her early start—becoming a mother as she turned eighteen—hasn't stopped her from being the best mum she can be. It does explain the seven-year gap between baby one and two, though. And much has happened in that time. She and Steven got married. Steven found a local trade, and my sister has been taking online courses. After Dad died they bought a house just three streets away from my Mum and thus secured the rest of Anna's life in Blaneswater.

After more tea and more cake, Tiffany looks awkwardly between Anna and me. Anna starts frantically shaking her head, but Tiffany has the face of a young woman who has made up her mind. She's got a plan, and she's going for it.

I know exactly what's coming.

"Auntie Carrie," Tiffany begins in a voice that belongs to a much older child, "why didn't Uncle Karl come to stay with you?"

Both Mum and Anna clear their throats and each starts as if to reprimand her, but I gently lift my hand, signalling that it's okay.

"Erm…" I think for a second. I haven't actually said any of this out loud yet. "Uncle Karl and I aren't together anymore, so it's just me now."

Her little face looks confused. "But don't you love each other anymore?"

Mum and Anna's wide eyes dart between Tiffany and me.

I want to laugh a bit. How do you explain a year and a half of not talking to each other to a child? Or him losing himself on his phone to women from work and old college girlfriends and basically anyone but me? Or him planning a future that doesn't have me in it?

"Uncle Karl just stopped loving me, sweetie," I said with a deep sigh. I don't know if I want to cry or not. I don't know if this was a fact that I'd been ignoring for over a year and saying it out loud is cathartic. Or maybe I just wanted to run into the street and scream until my lungs hurt.

She looks to Anna with eyes welling up. "Will you and Dad stop loving each other?" she asks and her little voice makes a squeak that actually makes her sound younger for the first time ever.

"No, sweetie," Anna says. "Uncle Karl was a prick. Your Dad's just silly sometimes."

Mum clears her throat at the sound of a curse word. Anna nods and gets to her feet. "Swear jar, I know, but this one was deserved." She ruffles my hair on the way by, acting as if she's the older sister when I've actually got two years on her.

"Auntie Carrie," Tiffany says, giggling as her mum drops a pound coin in a jar next to the fridge. "I still love you a lot."

"Thanks, sweetie," I say with a smile. I wish it was a real smile. I wish I could settle for the love of a niece who's just discovered the joys of Matilda and The Witches for the first time instead of missing the prick who didn't say more than a few sentences to me for the last six months of our five-year relationship.

When Anna eventually decides that it's time to haul her pregnant ass home (her belly is getting so big now), we discover that both the smoke and the Sister has returned. When we step outside, she tries to rush Tiffany into the car.

"Don't look at her, honey," Anna says as she fumbles with the booster seat.

Tiffany looks across the street anyway. Sister Smoke is amongst the ruins today, floating behind the remains of a window. There's no glass anymore, just a warped and melted frame. The white sheet that hangs over her body is all soot and smudges.

"She looks sad," Tiffany says as Anna helps with her seatbelt. "Like Auntie Carrie."

This is what my life has become. My niece comparing me getting left by my selfish boyfriend to the ghost of a woman whose cheating husband burnt her alive.

More weeks of pretending everything is fine go by. I manage to get myself back to work, taking the train from our tiny town through to the city. My boss had been kind by letting me take annual leave when I moved back into Mum's house. I work in software development for an educational company—making sure their learning materials work for schools, no matter how shitty the school's computers are. Most of my days are answering support tickets from distressed teachers. *Have you tried turning it off and on again?*

It's boring work, but it's steady work. Another thing Karl hated, though. He was convinced I had no ambition and didn't want better for myself. But when I worked on my own projects—coding little games from home—it was always a stupid pipe dream that I was wasting my time on. So which one was I? Not ambitious enough or ambitious about the wrong things?

As I take the train home, previous arguments spin in my head. I scroll through my Instagram feed, trying to push it away, but I land on a picture of him. Karl, sitting beside a group of co-workers in a bar. He's got his arm around a woman. One of the ones he used to spend all his time texting. Tears push their way out and I turn into one of those sad saps who sit and cry on public transport.

I arrive at the station in Blaneswater and walk mindlessly towards Mum's house, imagining things I should have said during fights or even during periods of the silent treatment. I imagine sending clever, sassy texts. I imagine simply sending links to breakup songs—the kind that say, "I don't need you, you dick." I imagine...

The sound of kids laughing and yelling grabs my attention and I look up to see that not only am I practically home, but the ash has started to fall again. It wasn't falling when I got off the train, but I can't tell for sure when it began. I was pretty deep down a pity spiral to notice. I fumble with my keys, but the obnoxious yelling is getting louder.

"Yeah, get her!" I hear and I spin around, stupidly convinced teens are about to mug me.

But it's not me they're yelling about. It's Sister Smoke. She floats high above the ruins, and a group of three teenagers—two boys and a girl—are laughing at her. The boys are picking up rocks and fragments of rubble to throw at her. The girl hasn't stepped onto the lot but is laughing from the broken streetlight.

Above the lot, the Sister floats. Ash drifts down from her once-white sheet. Fingers twitch.

"Ohmygod," the girl laughs in one breath. "Guys, don't! What if she gets you?!"

One of the boys turns. He's got floppy brown hair and he looks so familiar it hurts. There's a sideways smile on his face that he knows makes the girl weak at the knees. He's got her in the palm of his hand. His buddy is just there to make him look even better, recording the whole thing on his phone.

"Sarah, she does nothing. What are you scared of?" he says with a smugness that makes me feel sick.

Part of me wants to walk back in the house. But then I hear a stone hit her with a horrid *thunk*. That's enough.

"Oi!" I shout, and all three instantly turn. "What the fuck do you think you're doing?" I'm angrier than I thought, and the buddy runs off immediately. Floppy hair and the girl don't though. She looks at him as if seeking permission to leave.

Floppy hair doesn't move and stays where he is, practically on the porch of the ruined house. The girl is still under the lamppost and I stop my charge right next to her. I don't step onto the grounds of the Smoke Sister's home.

"What do you care, lady?" he asks, bouncing another piece of burnt brick in his hand. His hands are dirty from picking through the mess. "She's dead. Even she doesn't care."

I want to laugh. "Of course she cares," I spit at him. "Why do you think she comes back?"

"Whatever," he says with an eye roll, and throws another brick. This time the Sister isn't above the house. He looks lost as his projectile lands with an ineffective thud in the garden behind the lump of rubble. I see her move past one of the lower windows but don't say anything.

"Do you even know her story?" I ask, knowing full well that two fifteen-year-olds don't give a damn about a local legend. They just want something cool for their Snapchat.

The floppy haired boy is looking around for her now. He's only half listening. Even if I don't say anything else, I reckon I've scared him enough. But I don't want to stop yet. I focus on the girl, who shakes her head at my question. She's grasping her phone like it's a security blanket.

"The woman who lived in this house discovered that her husband of twenty years had a mistress. When she confronted him about it, he acted as if she was lying and making it up, and claimed that he wanted a divorce. Couldn't live with a madwoman like this who called him a liar all the time. And, while he was at it, she could get out—go live with her mother for all he cared.

"But she decided, nope, I'm not the one who messed up here. It's him. When he went to work the next day, she had the locks changed and got ready to wait him out. And that's when he got stupid. For some idiotic reason, he decided the way to get her out would be to frighten her out with a fire.

"Husband sneaks back one night, pours petrol through the letterbox and sets a fire. *Whoosh*! In no time at all, the fire is out of control and the woman is trapped. When the fire brigade arrived, they pulled her charred corpse out of the ruins of the house and she was obviously dead. They draped a sheet over her and the police carted the husband off.

"That night, the whole town was full of smoke and ash and the stench of death."

The girl's eyes are full of tears and I think I've definitely gotten through to her.

"That's stupid," the boy calls out, picking his way over the remains of the building, still looking for the ghost. "Why didn't she just jump out the window."

"Ohmygod," the girl gasps. "Shut up, Jacob."

"And anyway," the boy says. "If you know everything, Mrs Obsessed-With-the-Dead-Lady, why is the house still here? Why wouldn't they just knock the last of it down and build something new? Maybe she'd stop turning up if there was no house to haunt."

I smirk a little. Now I've got him. "Don't you know?" I ask, looking at him like he's not privy to a widely known secret. "Every time someone steps foot on the lot, she burns them."

The boy spins around and gives me the sideways smile he flashed the girl. He thinks he's caught me. "If that's true, why am I not on fire right now?"

I spot her, and I smile. "Because she hasn't touched you yet."

The girl sees her too. "Jacob," she whispers, and points behind him.

Jacob turns around slowly to find himself face to face with the remains of Sister Smoke. He screams wildly and runs, tripping over exposed brick and debris. He falls twice. He's gone before I can even laugh.

The girl doesn't move though. She stays rooted to the spot and watches as the Sister glides towards us. Toes scrape along the seared grass. I can hear the girl gulp down air in a panic.

"She won't touch us," I whisper. "We're on the road."

The girl looks down and realises that I've gently pulled her off the pavement and into the street. No cars are anywhere to be seen. We're safe.

Before us, the Sister hovers under the bent streetlight. There's a soft rasping of breath and the sheet flutters where her mouth is. There's a dark smudge where her eyes should be. Fingers flutter and spasm. Her head jerks and Sarah jumps beside me. We three women stand in the quiet of the evening and the smoke drifts around us. Eventually, I come to my senses and lean in to the girl.

"He'll pull you down and you won't even notice him doing it until you're too deep," I say. She nods, never taking her eyes off of the Sister. "Go home."

She does, and so do I.

*

That night, I call Anna. She's only a few streets away, but she's so close to giving birth now that I don't want to bother her with an actual visit. I lie on the bed and dial.

"Hi, what's wrong?" she answers. This is how we both always answer phone calls since Dad died. Never, "how are you?" Always, "what's wrong?"

"Everything's fine. You're not in bed, are you?" I ask, looking at the time. It's half past ten, but I'm aware that that's late for a pregnant lady with a small child.

"No, no," she answers. "Just doing the pre-bed clear up. Dishwasher, clothes in the basket, etc, etc."

"Eugh," I groan. "Such a grown-up."

"You're more grown than me," she retorts.

"Yeah, but now I'm one of those lives-with-mum losers."

"You're not a loser."

"I'm a bit of a loser."

"Not that I don't love these chats, but what's wrong?"

"Just a weird day," I sigh. "And I wanted to ask you something."

"What?"

"Remember when Sister Smoke burned you?"

"I've got a scar that won't let me forget it."

"I don't think you ever told me the full story when it happened. I just know you went onto the lot and she grabbed you."

There's silence on the other end of the phone. Then a tutting sound and another groan. I think Anna's attempting to sit down.

"What's brought this on?" she asks, avoiding what I've actually asked her.

"Just… some kids were being a dick to her today, and it was probably the closest I've ever been to her, and I was just wondering what it was like with you. The kids didn't know her story, and I wound up telling it. It's just got me thinking. Because… I don't know. I keep seeing her just now."

"Have you noticed when?" Anna asks.

The question takes me by surprise. "What do you mean?"

"Oh my god, Carrie," she laughs. "You can't be telling me that you did your spooky ghost story bit and then missed the whole moral of the tale?"

"I think I'm missing something massive."

"Okay. When I found out I was pregnant with Tiffany, I was pretty sure my life was over. I had literally just finished school and, if I'm brutally honest, I think Steven was on the verge of breaking up with me until he found out I was pregnant. I felt like shit.

"On the night I told Steven—over text message, true teenager style—I went outside and the smoke was there. I went for a walk, not really focusing on where I was going, and somehow I ended up in the old house. Like actually in amongst the rubble. Obviously, I started to panic. And I was crying my eyes out because I was pregnant, my boyfriend was acting like he wanted to dump me, and now I was sure that a ghost was about to kill me.

"She didn't kill me though. She stood in front of me and stared me down and, I swear to God, I could see her whole face through the sheet, and she was crying. Crying with me and crying for me. Then she reached out really slowly, and I had plenty of time to run away, but I didn't. Instead, she took my arm and held it.

"Granted, it hurt like fuck and now I have a horrible scar that I have to hide under long sleeves. But she made me feel safe, like I was going to be okay. I decided that night that I was going to be the greatest mum on the planet, no matter whether Steven was there or not. My life was not over. It was just different now."

"Have I missed this magical moral you were wanting to tell me here," I ask, trying not to cry again as I think about how brave my little sister was and still is.

"You're an idiot and you can work it out yourself."

"Thanks," I laugh. "Hey, I love you."

"I love you, too. And I meant it when I said that Karl was a prick."

"I know."

"Good, now I'm going to bed since this baby has stopped punching me and I might actually get some sleep."

"Good night."

She hangs up, and I put my phone down. I don't pull the blinds down tonight. The smoke has stopped, but it could start again any minute.

*

It's been two months at Mum's house now. I've fallen into the habit of work, hunting for a new place to stay, and waiting for Anna to announce that her water's broken. I've also stopped messaging Karl.

As if right on schedule, while on the train home from work, I get a text message from Mum all in caps saying, "BABY COMING!!!" This is also my sign to take my sad ass back to the house and wait. Mum will be at the hospital, hanging in a waiting room with Tiffany while Anna welcomes baby number two into the world. And I guess Steven will be there too, or whatever.

I'm excited for her, and I wait in the house impatiently. Trying to distract myself, I alternate between reading a paperback thriller and watching a reality tv show. Neither are very good, but they're addictive enough to soak up some of my time.

Three episodes into Britain's Pushiest Mums (incredibly sexist and exploitative, but I can't take my eyes off of it), there's a knock at the door. Fright inexplicably fills me. The irrational thought that Sister Smoke has finally crossed the street flits through my head before I knock it back for being nonsense.

Pulling the door open, I'm slapped with about twenty different emotions as I see Karl standing on my Mum's doorstep. There's a moment where it occurs to me that I used to kiss this person when I saw him. Instead, I freeze, not sure how to respond at all.

"Hi," he eventually says, and flashes an awkward smile.

"Hi," I respond, just as awkwardly.

"I thought I'd drop off some of your mail and some things you'd left," he says, handing me a huge canvas shopping bag full of what I can only describe as crap.

I'm still frozen. The man who broke my heart and then refused to speak to me is standing in front of me and acting like this is a normal thing he's doing. My heart is beating so hard that it hurts. I fear I may be having a panic attack.

Smoke fills the street behind him and flakes of ash start to fall. Karl looks up with a moment of confusion.

"Wow," he says. "I know you told me this happened but I didn't actually believe it. Jesus." He holds his hand out and the ash evaporates the minute it touches him.

Behind him, I see her. She's across the street, floating higher than usual. The jerking is more pronounced as well. I imagine that she nods at me.

I move my attention to Karl. His hair hangs over his eyes and it irritates me. I desperately want him to tuck it behind his ears. He doesn't.

"Why wouldn't you believe me?" I ask him calmly.

"Guess I just thought it was one of your crazy stories," he says, looking above him and letting his hand drift through the smoke.

"I've literally never told you a crazy story."

"Dead women in burnt-out houses seem pretty crazy to me."

"What are you actually doing here, Karl?" I say, pushing the conversation away from one where he continually calls me crazy.

"I just wanted to drop this stuff off. I saw that your sister had gone into labour so thought this was as good a time as any, before you're all neck deep in nappies."

How would he know about Anna? I trace my thoughts back and it occurs to me that I'd posted on Twitter. I can't call him on this since only a few weeks ago, I was rage scrolling through his Instagram feed.

"You mean, while nobody's here to call you out on being an asshole?" I snap. The Sister glides higher. She's practically standing on the streetlight now. I get it now. I know why she appears.

"No need to get nasty," he says, with that trademark smirk.

"No, you're just here to mess with my head. I'm doing better now and I can only guess one of your many 'harmless' flirtations are in a huff with you and you thought you'd come and see what you could get out of me?"

"That's not…"

"No, shut up," I order. "I'm done. You decided you were done with me and it turned everything upside down. I've lost my home and I've lost what I thought was my future. You can't come back here and try to fuck with me. I mean it. I'm done. You didn't want to talk and now neither do I."

He looks taken aback. I've never really spoken back calmly like this. Fights were always heated screaming matches. Not this.

"Goodbye, Karl."

Smoke thickens around him and he steps backwards off the porch. His car is parked across the road. He shakes his head and opens the door.

"You know," he begins, before getting in. "I was going to give you the chance to come back and see if we could fix this. See if it was worth saving."

My heart is set. The Sister moves her arms and the ash falls harder.

"It's not," I tell Karl firmly. "Now fuck off."

The Sister shrieks from her perch on the streetlight. Karl's head snaps round and he finally sees our neighbourhood ghoul.

"What the hell…"

"She's not a fan of lying men, Karl, so I'd get out of here while you've got the chance."

He scrambles into the car and fights with the ignition. She floats down and stands at the edge of the lot, practically at his car window.

"This town is as crazy as you," he yells out of the window as he stalls the car.

"I'd rather be a crazy bitch than a lying prick," I tell him, stepping down from the porch and walking across the pavement. "We're done, Karl. Goodbye."

The car sputters into life and he speeds off down the street.

I cross the road and stand on the edge of the Smoke Sister's damaged garden. She's a few feet from me and I can hear that rattling breath. Embracing the crazy that Karl had projected onto me, I step onto the grass. We're face to face now, and I can smell singed hair.

I think about what Anna said about that day back in her teens. The safety she described and I can feel it too. The Sister's hand twitches and I brace myself.

An idea comes to me first, though. I slowly reach out and take her arm. Just as Anna described happening to her. I take the corpse's arm and I tell her it will be okay.

She lets out a rattled sigh, and when I remove my hand, shards of burnt flesh come away. She's left with a pink handprint of flesh exposed. The ghost doesn't touch me and the smoke dissipates. I step off the lot and my phone buzzes in my pocket.

A text message from Mum: "IT'S A GIRL!!!!!!!"

When I look up from my phone, the Sister is gone.

I cry, but this time I'm happy. I'm happy for all of us.

EMMA KATHRYN is a horror fanatic from Glasgow, Scotland. You can find her on Twitter @girlofgotham. When she's not scaring herself to death, she is one half of The Yearbook Committee Podcast *or she's streaming indie games on Twitch. She is rather tiny and rather mad.*

WHITE NOISE

C.M. Lowry

April 28th

I'm lonely.

I'm stuck at the South Pole and the real world is a thousand miles away. Of course I'm lonely.

That's what I blame, anyway. I wasn't exactly Rudolph Valentino in normal society, but there's no hope for me out here. There's only four of us. Four! Me, plus three other humans. Not exactly the best odds for finding your one-in-a-million, is it?

It gets entirely hopeless when you look at the three in detail. There's Sylvia, Michelle, and Abdullah. Michelle is gay and Abdullah is a man—and I'm not that way inclined. That just leaves Sylvia. Happily married, twice-my-age Sylvia. Extremely slim pickings, in other words.

Don't get me wrong here—I know that you don't sign up to over-winter at Rothera Research Station for the social element. Not if you've got a brain, at least. And you probably have a pretty fine brain, given that it's a scientific research station. *The* scientific research station, if you are looking at the league tables of the British Arctic

Survey. It's a small list, and Rothera is the biggest by far. Not to mention the only one that's open all year round. Comparing them is like putting the Brazil football team in a penalty shoot-out against Warrington Town FC—there's an obvious winner. In fact, in summer there's usually over a hundred people on base. There are planes coming and going; the place hums like a weird frosty beehive, filled with strange, merino-fleeced insects.

Between March and October, though? The weather gets nasty—too nasty for flying, anyway. On the bad weeks, it's nearly too nasty to go outside at all. Visibility of less than a metre for days at a time. Not to mention the darkness. That's right—the sun sets... and stays there. For a month.

So why would anyone sign on to stay here? To be honest, I don't know. I didn't choose this, you see. I'm a fair-weather visitor, here to fiddle with the solar panels and sort out their data output. I was meant to get out on one of the last flights. But then, at the end of February, a storm came and just sat on top of the runway, and I missed my chance. The others saw it coming and got out on the last trip, but I was too busy trying to finish reviewing my data. Too busy, and too late.

I got even more lonely when the sun went away. More than I expected. The early winter didn't just trap *me* here, it stopped all the new staff from arriving. There were meant to be twenty-two people here over winter. Not four.

Just four. In the dark. Alone.

May 3rd

I was okay through March and April. Okay, not great. But it's May now, and they say the earliest we can get out is likely to be October. Six more months. I mentioned to Sylvia that I was feeling a bit low, and she arranged a video chat for me. One to one with Doc P, the psychologist at HQ. He was a bit condescending, really. "Start a journal, that'll help," he said. Dismissive.

Still, I'm trying it. We'll see if it helps.

May 18th

It's just so dark now, that's the problem. Night, day—there's barely any difference. Sure, sometimes we get the Southern Lights, but I don't know. There's something just too alien about them. Inhuman.

When you look into the sky and see a ghostly blue-green glow, everything just seems disconnected, somehow. As if we don't matter. Out here, our actions seem meaningless. Inconsequential.

Must say, not sure this journal is helping much. I don't feel any better. I don't feel anything. I am without consequence.

May 27th

I. Can. Not. Believe it! The only thing I had going for me was the internet. Communication with the outside world! The storm just ripped off our satellite dish. The mountings seem to have got loose, and the strong wind just tore them off. Gone!

"What about the backup?" I hear you ask. Well, somehow that's down too. Something to do with the interface with the main system. I've had a look, but I can't seem to work out the problem. Abdullah had a look too, but he's more of a meteorologist than a programmer. I'm the only one here with the skills to fix it, and—as I keep telling them—it just seems to be broken.

What a pain. The only outlet I had was sending off the odd missive into the void.

Not that anyone responds to my emails. Not even Mum. Would it be that hard to reply? Just occasionally? To fling back the odd message, let me know that they care and they miss me?

Ah well, at least it means everyone else is as miserable as me. Sometimes feels like the rest spend all their time on video calls to their loved ones. Seems a bit out of order, actually. There's only four of us around, and the three of them can't spare a moment for their colleague? A bit cold.

I'm almost glad the satellite broke. I'm definitely not going to waste my time trying to fix the relay. Not if it'll just encourage everyone to ignore me again. Besides, I've been having some great chats with Michelle since it went down. She's a lot more fun than I had realised!

June 5th

Good news today! I've finally finished editing all the solar panel data. All done. I suppose there's other work I could be getting on with, but without access to the server back in the UK, there's not much I can do. Or that I want to do, to be honest.

I thought we might grow closer together as a group without the satellite. And maybe we have, but I still seem to be spending 23 hours a day on my own.

I suggested a film night last week. I put on *"The Thing"*. I thought it would make people laugh, y'know? Research scientists in Antarctica being picked off one-by-one by a mysterious monster? Sylvia opted out straight away. "Horror's not to my taste," she said. Fair enough, I thought. Although, I dunno, would it really have hurt to stay? Show a bit of team spirit?

The other two watched it with me, although they started chatting halfway through. I turned up the volume a few times, hoping that they'd get the message. Abdullah called out during a particularly good bit, "Mike! Can you turn it down?! Don't want the ice shelf to break free before the credits, do we?" Michelle laughed.

I walked out. They tried to talk me back, but I was too angry.

Might have over-reacted a bit, I'm not sure. I just... if you come to watch a film? Watch the film, right? How am I the odd one out for actually wanting to pay attention? I heard them laughing as I went to my room. Alone again.

June 21st

Today was a terrible day. Awful. The heating unit died. Kaput. Bang. Like the satellite dish. Abdullah had a look, but he seems to have got himself locked out of the system, so we can't get it to turn back on. I've had a look, but I'm no expert.

Abdullah looked at me when I said that. "You are an expert though, aren't you? I thought you were an infrastructure technician?" I laughed it off, but there was something about his behaviour, after that. I'll have to keep an eye on him.

Without heating, the temperature dropped like a stone. It is -17°C outside, after all. Of course, at Rothera there are always redundancies and secondary options, but the backup generator only has enough oomph to keep the kitchen and one set of sleeping quarters warm. We're all clumped together in Sylvia's room at the moment, cocooned in layers of blankets. Quite cosy, really! At first it was a bit awkward, but by the end of the night we were laughing away. Michelle told us all a story about the shower pump freezing at Halley Station, and a mini iceberg forming in the bathroom unit. Hilarious.

I definitely wouldn't mind visiting the showers with Michelle. I know I'm not her usual flavour of romantic partner, but, well. Things can change. "Never say never" and all that. She definitely touched my arm earlier, for longer than was strictly necessary. Interesting.

Abdullah was watching us. Probably jealous. He seems the type.

July 2nd

Still no heating. Abdullah keeps trying to fix it. In the end, I've had to disable his access to the system. Can't have him accidentally breaking something else, can I? Could be disastrous.

He came to me about half an hour after I deleted his account. "Mike, my login has stopped working. Can you reset my password?"

I pretended to fiddle with things on my screen, and said, "There you go, should be sorted now."

Five minutes later he was back, "Sorry Mike, still not working. I don't understand why the system would lock me out, anyway. There's only us here?"

I sighed, and looked round the monitor, "Look Abdullah, I'm afraid I'm busy, I really need to focus on my work at the moment. Can you see if it starts working later?". I didn't wait for a reply, and turned back to my screen. I might only be playing Minesweeper, but it doesn't mean I have to be at his beck and call.

Felt like he closed my door a bit harder than was strictly necessary as he left. Rude.

July 3rd

Abdullah came to me five times today. FIVE. Asking me to activate his account. Get the hint already! Some people need to accept their place.

Eventually, I snapped, "Look, I don't know what's wrong with your account! Leave me alone!"

He glared at me, that same suspicious look I've been seeing more and more. "Mike, I know that you have disabled my account. I don't understand why, but we need to fix the satellite and the heating. That's your job, but you haven't done it, and you are obstructing me when I try to help."

I laughed at him. Me—obstructive? Ridiculous!

He left after that. I hoped for a bit of peace, but then, not five minutes later, Sylvia comes into my office. Apparently there have been "some complaints". She worded it carefully to make it sound like they were general complaints from various people, but it's obviously Abdullah. He'd just been in with me. And why would Michelle complain about me when we've been getting on so well?

I apologised for "the confusion" and immediately activated Abdullah's account again. Sylvia thanked me and left.

Twenty minutes later, I heard the heating tick on. It seemed that Abdullah had managed to fix the issue. Great.

A few minutes later there was a squeal of excitement down the hall. I poked my head out of my office. Michelle was hugging Abdullah, "You fixed the internet! Thank you! I never thought I'd be so happy!" Abdullah was smiling as he hugged her. I ducked away, before he made eye contact with me.

There was a party atmosphere in the station for the rest of the day. Michelle spending an hour laughing with her girlfriend on video chat. Sylvia speaking to her children. Whilst I had no one. Again.

July 5th

He's gone too far this time. I was reading through Abdullah's emails—I've had to put a filter on the outgoing SMTP server to stop things going out without my say so. Just in case.

Well, it's just as well that I did. He's contacted his boss and claimed that I had something to do with the breakdowns. Reported "suspicious" behaviour on my part! When he's the one who has been staring at me? Jealous of Michelle and me!

He says he's going to share all his concerns and evidence with Sylvia tomorrow. Apparently he has "proof" in the code I've written. Code he shouldn't have been able to see, if he'd just accepted the situation and stopped interfering.

This won't do. I'm not going to be all alone, I'm not going to let him take Michelle from me, and I'm not having my career put in jeopardy by someone so petty.

This won't do.

July 6th

Abdullah went missing last night. He left a computer printed note. Suicide. Terrible shame.

Now, I'll not pretend I'm overly sad to see him go. We never got on particularly well, but that doesn't mean you want to see someone dead! Gone, yes, out of your life. But not dead.

Sylvia announced the news at 7am. She called us into the break room.

"Guys, I'm not sure how to say this. I've found a note from Abdullah. It's..." her voice cracked, "...it's bad."

She handed it to us. We read it in silence. It was quite long, and a bit waffly, to be honest. Went on and on about not being good enough, about his insecurities. Very non specific, very sad. Michelle was in tears. I had to pretend to feel a little more upset than I was.

Sylvia gave Michelle a hug. Sly! Thought the old woman was married, but she seemed to enjoy the closeness with our young, pretty colleague. Wish I'd thought of it first.

At the end of the note, Abdullah said, "I'm going outside into the storm. Don't bother looking for me, it's too late."

Michelle was still weeping. I patted her hand, comfortingly. She looked blearily up at Sylvia. "What do we do?"

"Is there any way to access the door opening records?" said Sylvia to me. "If we know which way he went, we could look for him."

"Surely it's too late?" I said, reasonably. "He's probably been gone for ten hours or so. No one could survive that long out there..."

With a sniff, Michelle spoke up: "I was with him until about 1am, so it can't be more than five or six hours..."

"You were with him at one in the morning?!" I said. Surely they wouldn't have... Michelle wouldn't have... not with *him?*

"We had a couple of beers to celebrate the internet coming back," she said. "He seemed so happy... not, not like this." The tears started again.

Sylvia was looking at me again, "Well Mike, can you find out which way he went?"

"Sure", I said. I walked back to my room. Easiest to check on the terminal in there. The thought occurred that I might suggest a door on the *opposite* side from where Abdullah had left... and then I realised Sylvia was keeping pace with me. Why was she here? Was she checking up on me?

She looked fraught, the lines on her face deeper than they had been yesterday. "Thanks for this, Mike. With any luck, we won't be too late. What a terrible day." I muttered some kind of vaguely affirmative statement.

We arrived at my terminal, and I quickly accessed the records. We were all in Bransfield House, the newest building on site. I pointed to the line on the screen. "The database clearly shows the rear doors opening at 3:20am. That's four hours... in this." I gestured at the window; any view was hidden by a swirling interference of wind and snow. A world of white noise.

"Four hours isn't impossible at all," said Sylvia. She seemed happier. Hopeful. "He may be wrapped up well, or have taken shelter in one of the other buildings. We have to try!"

Ten minutes later the three of us were outside, wrapped in thick orange BAS parkas, armed with short-wave radios and warm flasks. Pointless, if you ask me. All around us, for hundreds of miles in every direction, nothing.

We wandered around aimlessly for an hour or so. There were no footprints left by the scouring winds, and we dared not travel more than a few metres from the station buildings. Eventually Sylvia announced it was time to head back inside.

We'd found nothing.

July 13th

It's been a week now, and I think the others have finally given up on finding Abdullah. I said it was hopeless at the time! He's definitely dead.

The mood here is even worse than it was before. I thought things would be more fun without him glaring at everyone all the time. But Michelle just keeps crying, and Sylvia seems sort of unsettled. She kept us searching for five days, long after Michelle had accepted he was gone. Pointless.

Even though Sylvia's stopped us going outside, she seems to have picked up some nasty habits from Abdullah. She looks at me strangely now. I catch her glaring across the break room. She looks away.

And she seems to be following in his footsteps in more than one way—she's been fiddling around in the system—looking at things she shouldn't. Bit harder to stop her; she's got an administration account. I've had to be a bit clever there. I don't mind her accessing the heating, weather, doors, all that, just as long as I get a say over the emails she sends out. Just in case.

August 1st

Things have carried on being awkward. Even more lonely. Michelle has withdrawn into herself even more. Doesn't smile or chat to me at all, these days. Nothing. I offered her a back rub on Thursday and she called me a creep! I blame Sylvia for that—she seems to have turned her away from me.

I sometimes walk into the kitchen whilst they are both there, and the conversation just stops. Dead.

"Hi gang, what you up to?" I ask. Big smile.

"Oh, you know. Just cooking dinner, that sort of thing," they reply. Even when they half smile back, it doesn't reach their eyes.

I know they are up to something, of course. I don't trust them. Not Sylvia, anyway. Without her around, I'm sure Michelle would be her friendly self once more. That spark, that undeniable spark we had? It just needs a little bit of warmth to let it shine. Sylvia is too cold.

August 6th

She was looking at the door access data today. Sylvia. I almost didn't bother checking, but given that I'm monitoring her screens now, I thought I'd have another look. Better than another game of Minesweeper.

Jolly glad I did too. You see, I forgot that the records wouldn't just show Abdullah leaving at 3:20am. It shows the doors opening again,

43 minutes later. The sort of time frame it would take someone to drag a body out, and hide it deep in the snow where no one would ever find it, no matter how hard they looked.

I went to her rooms. The door was open. Still on the computer. The room lights were off. She was lit with a ghostly blue-green glow.

"Hello Sylvia," I said.

She jerked round, surprise in her eyes. "Mike! What are you doing in here?" In front of her, the door access data was still displayed. 4:03am. I could see the incriminating record. It had been a mistake leaving that in place.

Easily resolved, though. She saw me look at the screen, and glanced back at it. A different expression now. Guilty. She knew she'd been caught out.

"What have you found? What have you done, Sylvia?"

Her email account was open. She been ready to tell someone!

The wide-eyed look was still there. I saw the moment she decided to act, as she lunged for the scissors on her desk. Yes, that's right. She attacked me! Awful, really. Not content with interfering in my relationship with Michelle, she escalated to physical assault!

I was ready, of course. I'm not a big man, but I can handle a middle-aged woman. It took me a while, but I put her somewhere safe, hidden from searching eyes. Took me less than 43 minutes this time, too.

A difficult day, but inevitable.

We're all safer now.

August 25th

This journal does seem to have helped. I'm still lonely sometimes, but it's not as painful as it was.

Part of that is because Michelle keeps me company, obviously. She doesn't talk much, but that's fine. It's nice. We sit together, comfortable. A companionable silence. One of the best relationships I've ever had, in some ways. I wouldn't say it's love, exactly, but it's a lot better than being alone.

Of course, I have to keep her in one of the other buildings. Too warm in here for her. Wouldn't be right. Wouldn't be pleasant, if you catch my drift. But we make do. I put on plenty of layers and we sit together.

Once you get down to it, it's not so bad really, Antarctica.

Not when you have someone to share it with.

*With special thanks to the **British Antarctic Survey** team on Twitter. @laura_gerrish and @efield_geo fielded some very odd is-this-guy-a-serial-killer type questions about Rothera Research Station.*

C.M LOWRY is an author based in Warrington, UK. He has a deep appreciation of board games, punk rock, and his family. And trifle. Find him at allaboutchris.org or on social media as @cmlowryauthor.

THE ECHO

Jelena Dunato

Annie's scream wakes me up.

It's not the snivelling of a five-year-old calling for her mother because she's had a bad dream, it's a full-grown, blood-curdling wail.

I jump out of bed and run down the corridor. Splinters from rough floorboards snag at my bare feet. Her door seems impossibly far, the corridor eerily twisted and uneven. When did the house turn into such a wreck? Sheets of bloated wallpaper hang from the walls, flecks of paint peel off the cracked window frames, thick layers of dust cover the furniture. It's been only two years since her father left. Is it possible that everything fell apart so quickly?

She screams again, and I run like the wind, like a storm rushing down from the mountains. Pale moonlight seeps through the holes in the dirty window panes, illuminating my path. I step on a glass shard, stumble and run on, leaving a trail of blood. My daughter is calling for me and I'm unable to cross the corridor that divides us.

Then I hear another voice from her room. The words are muffled, but I recognise its low, rumbling timbre immediately. The cold blade of fear pierces my gut and sets off a futile cry that dies on my lips. There's no one to answer my call for help.

I slam into her door and break into the room, calling Annie's name. A huge, hideous dark shape looms above my daughter, squeezing her tiny body, choking her.

"Leave her alone," I screech.

The sound makes the creature lift its head and moonlight reveals my ex-husband, his features disfigured by rage. Bulging, bloodshot eyes, bared teeth, saliva foaming at the corners of his mouth—all reason, all humanity gone from his face. Horror and panic explode in my chest, propelling me onwards. I crash directly into him without slowing down, desperate to get him off her.

He's twice my size and he swats me away like an annoying fly, throwing me to the other side of the room. My head hits the wall with a sickening crunch. I must have bitten my tongue, because the metallic taste of blood fills my mouth. But he's turned away from the child and let go of her neck, and that's all that matters.

Annie fights for breath, coughing and wheezing softly. I want to run to her, take her in my arms, protect her from this beast who turned our lives into a nightmare. He stands between us, his head nearly reaching the mouldy beams I painted yellow a lifetime ago. He's grown a beard, I notice, and his hair is long and filthy. White organza curtains splattered with dirt and torn into ribbons flutter in the wind, reaching for him like ghostly fingers.

"I planned to deal with you later," my ex-husband says. "But you always have to spoil my plans."

The child behind him makes no sound. She tries to make herself small, invisible. That won't help her, though. It never has. I have to lure him away.

"Catch me if you can," I say, wiping the blood off my lip.

He lunges, but I'm ready. I fly out of the room and run down the nightmare corridor again. There is a monster behind me: not a figment of some writer's imagination, but the man I married. The man who spent two years in prison because he broke his daughter's collarbone and two ribs.

What fool let him out without warning?

As I reach the stairs, he catches up with me and grabs my nightgown. Instead of tearing away, I cling to him and jump into nothingness. We roll down the stairs together, breaking off pieces of the rotten banister. We crash on the landing, stunned. My whole body hurts, but I think nothing's broken. He growls like a bear shot full of pellets. He's out for the moment, though it won't last long.

I use the respite to run for the kitchen. I push the door open and a horrendous odour of decay fills my nostrils. The kitchen is an awful wreck. Cabinet doors hang from broken hinges, smashed plates cover the floor. The fridge is open, full of putrid food. Something slimy grows in the sink. There's no time to gawk, though, for the sound of his footsteps echoes in the corridor, coming closer.

I rush towards the knife drawer and pull. Nothing happens; it's stuck. I shake it, praying and cursing in the same breath. He limps closer. No words, just heavy panting and the stench of old sweat and grease that surrounds him. The drawer finally gives in and I grab the first knife that comes to hand. I turn, but it's already too late.

The blow connects with my jaw and throws me backwards, onto the countertop. He charges at me with a growl, a mountain of muscles and menace. The knife in my hand comes to life and sinks into his upper arm, grating against the bone. I try to pull it out while he screams in pain and fury, but the blade won't come out of the flesh. One precious second passes, then another, before I let go of the handle. He wraps his other hand around my neck and squeezes.

Unable to breathe, I sink to my knees. His wounded arm joins his good one. He grabs my head, slams it into the cabinet. The first impact hurts like a red explosion, the second makes my vision sink into darkness, and the third one is just a muffled noise in the background.

My feet slip on the floor; I cannot get a hold. There must be some way to escape him, to stop him. There *must* be. The knowledge that I cannot protect my daughter is worse than hell. Terror grips me. Will I die like this, in this house in the middle of nowhere, with my child upstairs and a murderous psychopath in the kitchen?

I fight with the last atoms of my strength, clawing at his face, trying to scratch his eyes out. He's stronger than me. With every new blow, I'm further from escaping him. I wish I had stabbed him in the neck or chest. Would it make a difference? Is there a single scenario where I can stop him?

Is there…?

And then I realise. I remember. Rolling down the stairs, jumping through the window, running into the kitchen, running into the bathroom, running out of the house, a knife to the arm, a meat fork to the thigh, a pair of scissors stuck into his chest. All are variants of the same event and they all end the same. There is no happy end.

I've died like this a thousand times.

Remember, I scream at myself as I slip out of this world.

Annie's scream wakes me up.

It's not the snivelling of a five-year-old calling for her mother because she's had a bad dream, it's a full-grown, blood-curdling wail.

I jump out of bed and run down the corridor. Splinters from rough floorboards snag at my bare feet. Her door seems impossibly far, the corridor eerily twisted and uneven. When did the house turn into such a wreck? Sheets of bloated wallpaper hang from the walls, flecks of paint peel off the cracked window frames, thick layers of dust cover the furniture. It's been only two years since her father left, is it possible that everything fell apart so quickly?

But no, I remember, it hasn't been two years. It's been twenty.

I pause in the corridor. I always run into her room, he sees me, and the race begins. We end up downstairs, where he kills me.

Not this time.

I pick up a long, sharp shard from the floor. I tiptoe to my daughter's room, her screams breaking my heart. My whole body shakes from the unbearable urge to rush to her.

I need to be quiet. I need to be fast.

Hunched over Annie, my ex-husband doesn't see me. I grab his shaggy hair and its rancid stench hits my nostrils. He roars in surprise.

There's no time to waste. The shard cuts my fingers, but it doesn't matter because before he can move, I cut his throat. Hot blood spills over my fingers and sprays across my daughter's bed.

He jerks a couple of times and then his body becomes heavy and limp. I push it away.

"Mama?" my daughter whispers. Her eyes are huge, incredulous.

"Annie." I take her tiny, cold hand. "It's over."

As I say the words, a light appears in the window. Not the sickly silver moonlight, but bright yellow sunlight, melting everything it touches: the peeling walls, the rotting floorboards, the broken furniture. I grab my daughter and whisper "I love you" just as it reaches my bare feet.

A wave of light washes over us, warm and tingling. I hold Annie tight—safe and unharmed for once. As we disappear, I know we're finally free.

————◁◆▷————

JELENA DUNATO is an art historian, curator, speculative fiction writer and lover of all things ancient. She grew up in Croatia on a steady diet of adventure stories and then wandered the world for a decade, building a career in the arts and writing stories that lay buried in the depths of her laptop until she gathered the courage to publish them.

Jelena lives on an island in the Adriatic with her husband, daughter and cat. You can find her at jelenadunato.com and on Twitter @jelenawrites.

CHARMING

Julie Sevens

Jenna stared at the notifications on her phone in disbelief, mouth ajar. "Mr Charming contestant found murdered," she read, three times before it sunk in. The phone started vibrating in her hand: gossips checking to see if she knew more; bosses demanding to know why she hadn't warned them of the news; and friends making sure she had heard.

She set her phone down on her barely used kitchen counter—gently, as if it might explode—and opened her laptop. Scrolling through her feed, she dumped stale wine into a coffee mug and sipped it, a hot pink stain blooming on the rim. Her phone buzzed against the polished white faux marble, and she peeked at it. "I didn't tell you because I didn't know either, dude," she whispered into the wine. Jenna smacked the cursor around the laptop's screen until a story that didn't break her ad blocker opened.

The familiar face of one of her contestants from last season splashed across the screen. Rachel had won the "lost slipper" challenge, where the girls had to entice Mr Charming to invite them on a date by sending a single, anonymous piece of clothing for him to choose from. Rachel had sent last year's fledgling prince an old concert t-shirt from his favourite band, and the audiences had eaten it up. It was a proud moment for Jenna, who had set Rachel up for the win by giving her the shirt to use.

Jenna had a soft spot for Rachel. She was spunky and fresh-faced, and looked great on camera. But she had also proven to be kind, refusing to gossip about the other contestants, offering hugs to women who were overwhelmed or upset even if the cameras weren't on them. She had been an instant fan favourite until she told Mr Charming that she wasn't sure if she was developing feelings for him in return, and he had cried into his carefully plated sushi. This had dramatically helped the show's ratings, but also sparked debate about Rachel's motives that Jenna knew she hadn't deserved.

Rachel had been destined to come back in a later season or spinoff show, and the headshot the news used looked like something Jenna might have sent out in a press kit under better circumstances. Below Rachel's picture, though, was the description of a bloody, messy crime scene. Jenna couldn't bear to think about what sounded like a lengthy, painful attack, taking another gulp of stale wine as she scanned through to see if there was any indication at all of who had broken into Rachel's house and killed her, or why. But instead there was just a number for a tip line.

Jenna drained the mug and texted her boss back, "We need to offer a reward. A big one." While she waited for a response, she curled up under the big blanket on her couch and turned on a rerun of The Soup. By the first commercial break, Jenna was sobbing.

*

"One day," Brother James bellowed. "One day we will look out over the fields, and the lifeless eyes of the unchosen will stare back at us. The green, grey, and red mass of the decaying will heave as it expels its last life. And we will be grateful. Yes! We will! We will be grateful to be the virtuous chosen!"

Brett quivered at the thought, imagining himself standing mostly alone, victorious, as the sinful fell to whatever they were due when it was all over.

The rows of pews were mostly quiet until the end, when they erupted in cheers and hollers, fists pumping in the air. Brett noticed that more and more of the seats were full lately, the front pews filling up in the old, red-doored church they had bought last summer when it was only the original twelve of them.

The appeal—to Brett it was very clear—was that those pews were empty of whining babies, fidgeting children, shushing mothers. The only members welcome were adult men, and only men who believed in being men. Brett forgot sometimes what it had been like to go to the church his mom dragged him to, but when explaining the Benjaminite Brotherhood to potential recruits, he would breathe deeply through his nose and describe the lack of distraction, the ability for the men to concentrate and be themselves. There was nobody to nag at them about their clothes or the violence of their message. There were no delicate ears around.

And then, the world making sense again after the Message, he would fling open the doors and make his new BMW chirp across the parking lot with his key fob, just because he could. Not only was his new church pretty fun, it was also proving to be pretty lucrative for the founding twelve members. It had been Brett's idea to focus on recruiting whales; lots of trust fund bros and inveterate bachelors with summer homes and boats. They fanned out to network at all the local golf clubs, befriending a certain kind of man who had realised what he wanted out of life and was angry not to get it immediately, inviting them to this boy's club. Then the fees and donations rolled on in, although many of the members weren't privy to the true mission of the Benjaminite Brotherhood, which wasn't the never-ending bachelor party it seemed to be.

Jenna liked to absorb the hugeness of the cavernous red marble entry hall before going up to her tiny windowless office for the day. Nobody in the library-quiet lobby ever spoke to her or needed anything from her, and she was tempted sometimes to let the elevator go without her and leave her a few extra minutes. Today, though, Jenna was in a rush, just as she had spent days in a rush, trying to get a memorial piece stitched together for Rachel that could air before tonight's episode.

Jenna tried her hardest to provide a snapshot of Rachel in the one-minute slot she'd been given. She emphasised the photos from the family and testimonials from her friends, instead of focusing on Rachel as part of the show. Mr Charming had been only a few months of her life, and it didn't feel right to make it about that. At the end,

Jenna taped herself as a representative of the show, pleading with the audience to call the tip line if they knew anything, to get justice for Rachel. It had taken her eight takes to get it right, the pressure of filming something that felt like it actually mattered getting to her. When she watched the episode on air, it still felt so short—too short— an attempt to wrap someone up in a 60 second package and hand it over to the audience.

The next morning, when her friend Taylor stopped by to convince her to eat lunch, Jenna gestured for Taylor to close the door instead. "I don't even know what to do with this, Taylor. A courier brought this up like twenty minutes ago." She tapped the envelope against the desk. "Read it."

Taylor reluctantly took the envelope, examining the outside. It was a regular manila envelope, a printed label from the courier service on the front. She unfolded the single sheet of printer paper that fell out, revealing a short note centred on the page in a ridiculous, loopy-cursive font. No signature, nothing to indicate who it was from.

She read it aloud: "Jenna—I saw you whining about how poor Rachel deserves justice, you stupid bitch. Did you ever stop to consider that she got justice? I made her apologise, but that doesn't fix what she did. Give us the respect we deserve—that's justice. Men are in charge and it's time for you to understand that before it is too late, and we all receive our final judgement."

Taylor let the letter drop in her lap, sighing quietly. "So, like, I know you probably want this to go away, but I think you should tell the leads. This isn't normal hate mail; this is pretty scary."

The threat of the letter hung in the air as one of the interns burst through the door.

"Guys—" He paused, sensing the mood in the room. Taylor turned to give him a death stare for interrupting them, but softened when she saw how distressed he was. "Another one of the women was killed last night. Emmie," he said, then turned his laptop screen around so they could see. "Mr Charming Turns Mr Sinister," the headline read.

"Yikes. That makes it sound like our actual dude became a serial killer on set." Taylor said, grimacing. The weight of another death settled over them, and she whispered, "Emmie, huh?" Emmie was another of the fan favourites that season, a strikingly beautiful woman with a fierce independent streak. "A second murder of one of the women right after air?" Taylor whispered to herself. Jenna stared, frozen, at the letter in Taylor's lap, her face blanched.

Brett soaked in all the articles he could find about his handiwork, relishing in the internet hot takes linking Emmie's violent end with her behaviour on the show. He was thrilled to see people starting to wake up; to wonder whether there might be consequences for acting like Emmie. Brett had been stunned when Emmie told Mr Charming she wouldn't respect his choices; that she wasn't sure she could move to Atlanta to be with him. Clearly, Emmie was not going to be a good fit for the Benjaminite Brotherhood's plans.

As he searched for even more articles, he came across a clip showing the producer from the memorial segment, and sat up straighter as he clicked play. When the camera panned over to Jenna, sitting there on the bright orange morning show couch, Brett clenched himself, ready to feel righteously angry at this chick who implied that his mission wasn't to bring more justice to the world. Then he noticed the bouncy waves in her hair; the tasteful, muted pink lipstick that matched her expensive-looking blazer.

The helmet-haired morning show host showed his letter on screen, taking a break from speculating about the effect of a serial killer on the show to ask Jenna if the show had any idea who may have written the letter. The host called him all kinds of disrespectful names— "sexist", "unhinged"—but he noticed that Jenna declined to agree with the host's accusations against him, instead explaining they didn't know who wrote the letter. Brett's heart swelled. This one might be worth saving if she understood his mission. He imagined himself soon towering over the ash heap of the world, but this time Jenna was at his side, smiling up at him lovingly, waiting for him to lead, to reshape the new world.

Jenna looked forward to a hot bath and a cold beer in her pyjamas as she rode the elevator up to her apartment. After taping the morning show, she had spent the day trying to put her own entanglement in the killer's web out of her mind and focus on a new memorial spot for Emmie. They couldn't air any more episodes of Mr Charming until the killer was caught, and honestly, it was unclear if they'd ever finish the season. But the network wanted a spot like Rachel's anyway, probably for an evening news show that would cover the murders.

In the elevator, Jenna rubbed her temples, thinking about Emmie's family. Rachel's parents had jumped at the chance to send photos and memories of Rachel, thanking Jenna over and over for the reward Mr Charming was offering. Emmie's brother, on the other hand, had answered her call reluctantly, telling her it was the show's fault Emmie was dead, and that they weren't going to participate in a PR stunt. Her brother said they shouldn't have aired the next episode after Rachel's murder, and Jenna struggled to respond, wondering if he was right.

As soon as she unlocked her door, though, she felt uneasy instead of relieved to be home. There was something off. A smell, maybe; subconscious evidence of an unfamiliar person. She flung the door wide and stood in the doorway, looking around, listening. Only the sound of her own breath quickening disturbed the silence. Leaving the door open, she backed down the hall to the door of the only neighbour she sort of knew, the man with the cute dog.

His dog went wild before she even knocked, and when he cracked the door, Jenna started: "Hey, so maybe I'm just crazy but I got this creepy letter at work and I just got home and it kind of feels like someone's been in my place and I was just wondering if maybe you'd help me make sure everything is okay, I am just so paranoid because of this work stuff…" She stopped herself, realising she hadn't really meant to say all that.

"Say no more. Sounds like you're having a rough day," he said, opening the door further. "Sadie's got a great nose, and she loves to visit new kitchens." He grabbed Sadie's leash, and she bounced back and forth on her front paws, slobbering. Jenna wasn't sure what a very adorable Boston terrier would do to protect them from a serial killer, but she was glad for the dog's company nonetheless.

"Thanks," Jenna smiled. She was sorry she knew Sadie so well but not his owner. He had serious high-school-math-teacher vibes, and she was glad he'd been home. They stepped back to her wide-open door and her neighbour peeked his head in.

"What do you think, Sadie, all clear?" The trio checked behind doors, in closets, under her bed. Sadie slobbered at something on the kitchen floor, but other than some crumbs they found nothing amiss— nothing like the smashed glass or strewn drawers Jenna had imagined.

"Those are nice flowers," the neighbour said, gesturing at her dining table. Jenna opened her mouth to say thanks, but froze when she saw the flowers he referred to. An ostentatious spray had taken over her little dining table, a basket the size of a hatbox brimming with lilies, mums, roses.

"I don't know where they're from," she said, to both of their dismay. Sadie sat down by her feet, pawing at her toes. Her neighbour furrowed his brow, unsettled, scanning the room again. They'd been focused on finding signs of a break-in, but now it was clear someone had been in her place for much more foreboding reasons.

"Do you have a friend or a boyfriend or anybody with a key? Maybe," he leaned in closer to the floral arrangement, separating the stems to find a card, "maybe it's from them." Jenna shook her head emphatically, scared to see the card in his hand. He slid it from its envelope and dropped it on the table, leaning over it.

"Should I read it to you?" he asked. Jenna sat down on the kitchen floor, giving Sadie a cuddle. She steeled herself, nodding. "Okay." He paused, taking a deep breath. "It says, 'Saw you on TV today. You look nice in pink. I'll be back'." He winced as he said the last part, shaken, his eyes on the pink blazer she still wore under her coat. "I think you should call the cops. This is really fucked up."

Jenna said nothing for a few seconds, pursing her lips. "Listen. I really appreciate your help, but I don't think I can tell anyone. I'll just go stay with a friend." She tried to smile convincingly, wishing she wasn't so personally part of this. "Do you think you and Sadie could just stay right here for a minute while I pack a couple things?"

Brett slammed his palms against his steering wheel, the car shaking with the force of his rage. He had been sitting outside Jenna's building in his Beamer for three hours waiting for her to get home, but he was willing to forgive her for making him wait. She had walked into her building a few minutes ago wearing a brown felt coat that looked soft, tied around her waist in a way that pleased him. Nodding his approval, he was glad he had found a woman who always dressed well, didn't let herself go. He'd never seen her in old sweatpants, a sloppy ponytail; he'd looked in her closet and even her pyjamas were classy. His heart had raced as he ran his fingers over the maroon satin, imagining her sleeping in them.

He had waited for her to appear upstairs, holding his breath for the reaction to the flowers he had left for her. They were the most expensive ones he could find on short notice, so he was sure she would love them. But then the lights had flicked on in her kitchen; a shadow on the ceiling as someone approached. He had gasped when a man appeared in the window, pawing through Jenna's flowers, his traitorous grubby fingers finding the card Brett had left.

Brett seethed with rage, his palms aching. How could Jenna have betrayed him like this? Why would she let another man into her apartment? He pictured the man in the window being allowed to watch Jenna slip those silken pyjamas slowly across her skin, and he thought he might explode.

The front door of the building opened, and Brett ducked when he saw Jenna and this arrogant asshole come out. She hefted a duffel bag into the seat of an Uber and waved to the other guy. Brett's thoughts scrambled as he tried to decide whether to follow her to win her away from this guy, or to confront the man who had betrayed him. His anger won, as it often did, and he slipped out of his car, crossed the street, and caught the door just in time to sneak back into the building. He followed the man into the elevator, facing forward at first, pretending to be an innocent elevator passenger. The man reached a finger out, pressing the button for Jenna's floor as the door closed.

Brett's fists flew into this snake-in-the-grass's face, a satisfying smash as his right hand connected. His tormentor yelped in shock, crumpling to the floor of the elevator. Brett kicked him as hard as he could, his foot thudding against ribs, shoulders, kidneys. He grabbed the railing for better leverage, to do more damage, out for blood. He had to pay for trying to claim Jenna as his territory. Brett had to make it known that Jenna belonged to him and him alone. He leaned down over his adversary, pressing his face into the floor of the elevator, watching blood drip from his nose into the dimpled grey rubber tiles. "Stay away from Jenna. She's mine."

The elevator dinged, and Brett hurried away down the stairs and out the back door of the building. He had sped away by the time an elderly woman wheeled a trolley full of groceries up to the elevator and pressed the button.

"Jenna, come sit down. You've been pacing in front of the window for ten minutes and your food's getting cold." Taylor waved her hand at the takeout containers scattered on her coffee table. She worried about Jenna, knowing she had barely slept since Rachel's murder.

"I'm just so wound up. It was so awful when Rachel died, but we didn't imagine it had anything to do with the show. And now Emmie is dead too, and her family said it's our fault, and I honestly don't know if I disagree. And this guy is apparently after me too? It's a lot." Jenna was bouncing on her heels, as dishevelled as Taylor had ever seen her. "I can't even find my hairbrush, look at me."

Taylor thought for a long second, wrapping noodles around her fork like a gear turning slowly. "We need to up our defences for sure. I mean, this guy, I doubt he knows you're here, but what if he shows up? I think the show should give you a bodyguard or something."

Springing from the couch, Taylor disappeared into the kitchen. Jenna tried to sit down and eat something, listening as Taylor rummaged through drawers. She came back ten minutes later with a maxi pad in her hand, presenting it to Jenna as if it were a diamond necklace. Jenna raised her eyebrow at it, then at Taylor.

"It's a disguised smart watch. I was listening to this true crime podcast the other day, and this mom found her kid alive after three days with find-my-phone. She was in a ditch after a car crash and they never would have found her." Taylor said, realising that the anecdote might be less comforting than she'd hoped. "Keep it with you, then I can find you! You have to promise you'll keep it charged."

"Aw, thanks. I will. You're a good friend, Taylor." She took the spy pad and tucked it in the little zippered pocket in her purse. At least it would help Taylor feel better.

"Hey, Brother Keith. Hey, man. I got this girl; she's driving me crazy. I found out she's been cheating on me, and she has to stop doing that, you know. Do you think I could borrow the cabin today?" Brett yelled towards the BMW's hands-free set. He liked his phone calls loud enough that you could hear them from outside the car, but for such a serious topic he turned it down a little.

"Yeah, sure, anything you need, Brother Brett. This girl doesn't sound worth the trouble though, are you sure she meets our criteria? She must look real good." Keith laughed, crackling on the speaker. "Listen, you know the code for the door. I haven't been up there in a few weeks, but I think you probably need some supplies so I'd stop by the store before you head out there."

"Thanks, I'll keep you updated. You're a champ." Brett hung up the call with a smile on his face. Keith had been a great recruit for the church. He was proving to be loyal and more importantly, he had a lot of assets. Extremely useful assets. Brett whistled as he glanced in the rearview mirror at the paper bag stuffed with Jenna's things. He wanted her to be comfortable during her stay at Chez Keith, and he knew she would appreciate how thoughtful he was to pack for her since she wouldn't have the chance to plan for her trip.

"Meet you at Rebar?" Jenna texted Taylor on her way out of the office, after another long day of dealing with the fallout of her show becoming a serial killer hunting ground. Their trusty bar was only a couple blocks away.

Taylor replied with a winky face, "Saved you a seat."

Jenna slid into her seat across the table from Taylor, tucking her feet up on the tall chair's rail. "So" she started, ripping off the band-aid, "Remember the neighbour who was with me when I found the flowers? The police came to talk to me today and Philip—his name is Philip, I feel so bad for forgetting his name—got beat up in the elevator when I left to come stay with you." Jenna wiped the condensation away from the copper mug, staring at her distorted reflection. She had wanted to keep the letter private, and ended up with the lead producers putting her on a morning show. Then she'd tried to keep the flowers secret and someone else had gotten hurt. Jenna felt trapped, like every choice she had made was the wrong one.

"Oh my god, Jenna." Taylor put her hand on Jenna's arm. They whispered for a few minutes, Jenna on the verge of tears. They paused as the server slid a fresh round of drinks toward them, trimmed with lime wedges and black paper straws. He took Jenna's empty mug away as she gulped at the second one. Taylor wanted her friend to know this wasn't her fault, but everything she said felt too small, like throwing pebbles in the ocean.

"Hold on, I have to pee. I'll be right back," Taylor said, leaving her fresh drink untouched on the table. Jenna pulled out her phone to scroll through Mr Charming news alerts, every story worse than the last. She started to feel woozy, her heart pounding unsteadily in her chest. She had trouble shoving her phone back in her purse with her clammy hands.

She climbed out of the chair, wondering why she felt so drunk halfway through her second drink, trying to remember if she had eaten lunch. Deciding to go find Taylor in the bathroom, she tried to get through the people waiting for a table, panicking a little, like an animal caught in a stampede, even though everyone else seemed to be having a good time. Her legs started to feel weak; her vision blurring at the edges.

Feeling a presence behind her, she tried to turn around. He put his arm around her waist as her knees buckled and said, "I've got you, I've got you. It's okay, Jenna." Brett's tone was an attempt at soothing, but it made Jenna's blood freeze. He led her through the happy-hour crowds at the door, her purse on his arm, just as Taylor came back to their table, looking around for her friend.

*

Jenna squeezed her eyes shut when she woke up, trying to turn herself back off, but reality held. She leaned over and threw up onto the concrete floor. Her hands wouldn't move to wipe her mouth; they were tied behind her back so tightly they were numb. It was cold, damp, and musty. She had no idea what time it was—the only light was a dim glow near the ceiling, behind the silhouette of some shelves.

Leaning back, Jenna tried to think. Her head pounded, the fog of whatever had made her unconscious not quite lifting. She remembered being at Rebar with Taylor, but that was it. Confused, disoriented, she wondered if she should know where she was. This was obviously a bad situation, and she knew she was in danger, but she just felt numbly confused.

A door abruptly opened near where she had imagined the ceiling, flooding what was now clearly a basement with light. Looking down, she realised she was wearing her own pyjamas, and was circled with a bizarre assortment: her missing hairbrush, her bottle of lotion, her dress laid out carefully on newspapers, her old water bottle. It was a strange shrine to herself, all these familiar things that she couldn't reach or use, and her skin prickled when she realised how he had gotten them.

"Good morning, sunshine!" Brett said when he reached the bottom of the stairs. "You woke up just in time. I was afraid I would have to have dinner with you while you were asleep!" Jenna studied him, wondering what her best chances of survival were, willing her brain to unjumble just enough to make it through this.

"Did you let my friend know we were leaving the bar?" she asked him, striving for a casual tone, trying not to stare at the things he had stolen from her apartment.

"No, she was in the bathroom when you needed to leave," Brett said. "You can have your purse back, but I took your phone and your pepper spray so we can really focus, you know?" He was staring intensely at her, waiting for her appreciation. "It's time for dinner, we're going upstairs now. Put your dress on." He stared at her, not planning to give her any privacy. She managed to change into the short, sequined dress the way kids change at slumber parties, clothes going on under a layer or over another like a quick-change magician, much to his disappointment.

"There you go, Jenna. Look, there's some aspirin, I bet you have a headache. I read online about the side effects of the drug you took." He gripped the base of her neck roughly with one hand. Pulling a chair away from the table with his foot, he shoved her down into the chair, and wrapped her in bungee cords and rope, this time leaving her arms free. Her wrists were mottled purple and red, and one of her fingernails was ripped. "That's too bad about your wrists, there. I worried you might try to leave before you got a chance to explain yourself to me." His voice took on a hard tone at the end, and he took a deep breath, balling his hands into fists as if to stop himself from something.

He clapped his hands together. "But let's have a fresh start, hey? Your dear Brett here really wants to give you another chance," he said, artificially brightly, that hard tone still lurking under the surface. Pulling the tin foil cover off a plate in front of her, he revealed what appeared to be a frozen pot pie, burned around the edges, on someone's grandmother's china. "I made us a nice dinner, now, and we have all the time in the world." He stared at Jenna until she took a bite. She pushed a shaking forkful into her mouth, nodding enthusiastically.

The table was dressed in a white tablecloth, four crystal candlesticks in the centre sparkling in their own light. It was set much the same way she might have set up a date for Mr Charming, arranged all for the cameras. The food would always be stale and cold by the time the contestants sat down, but as Jenna always told them, nobody was watching the show to see them eat, anyway. It seemed that Jenna was now on one of these fake dates, but with much higher stakes, and with someone who didn't seem to have a great grasp on the whole reality/fantasy distinction.

A car caught her eye, slow-motion creeping up the driveway out the window over Brett's shoulder. Jenna bit her tongue when she saw the stripes up the side, realising it was a police car. "This is really good, Brett. You must be a great cook!" She played along, taking a long sip of water from her champagne flute, hoping he would focus on her, trying not to imagine how he would react to the slowly creeping caravan of police cars following the first.

Brett met her gaze, suddenly suspicious. He turned around and saw the scene out the window. "What did you do?" he raged. "This was your last chance, and you ruined it! You ruined our date!" He leapt up, grabbing the back of her chair and dragging her and the chair across the room. He shoved her into a closet, slamming the door into her, bashing into the door until a chair leg snapped and the door clicked shut, trapping her jammed sideways against the closet wall.

He stomped out the front door, and she heard him screaming at the police. "You are on private property. This land belongs to the Benjaminite Brotherhood and you are all trespassers. I am TRYING to have a nice, quiet evening with my girlfriend." Brett sounded genuinely surprised the police weren't taking orders from him. "No, I will not lay in this dirt, I will not sully—" Jenna heard a zapping noise, followed by a thud, and then heavy boots outside the door.

In the closet, Jenna listened carefully until it was clear several people were inside the cabin, and not just Brett. "Help!" she screamed, surprising herself with the volume and intensity of the single syllable, the word not ending until she ran out of breath. The boots paused, and she yelled again. This time, she heard them all rushing toward the closet.

Brett pressed his lips against the mouthpiece of the pay phone. "I heard they're airing the rest of the season of Mr Charming now, Brother Keith," he whispered, nodding at the answer. "I can't say much, you know. The guards listen to these calls. I got so distracted by the wrong things. I lost sight of the vision of the Brotherhood. Make sure in your work, you know, you don't make the mistake I made. You have to follow through, stay on task, right, Keith?" He smiled into the receiver, "Uh huh, uh huh yep. You got it. Well, I'm with you in spirit. You'll be richly rewarded, I'm sure. Okay, time's up. Be careful, Keith."

He clanged the phone back on the hook, satisfied.

JULIE SEVENS is an Ohioan who transplanted to Philadelphia and Berlin before finally settling in the Chicago area with her husband and son. You can find more of her nightmares at juliesevens.com.

THE FOLLOWER:
OR PSALM 127:3
Andrew Joseph White

Saul wipes blood off his knife and asks Isaac to pray for the bodies. Isaac is over in the plush suburban living room, too busy staring at his no-fingerprint fingertips to hear. His hands still feel like they're pressed into the acid, erasing whorls of skin like an old self, burning a line between who he is and what he used to be. Or some poetic bullshit like that.

The thing that gets Isaac is, a little glass bottle of acid costs sixteen dollars. What also gets him is, you can buy enough acid to kill a man for sixteen dollars and Saul can kill a man for free. That's why Saul didn't want to buy the acid to burn off Isaac's fingerprints. Because Saul could just take a knife and do it his damn self. But cutting them off meant cutting them off ten times while acid meant you could do all ten at once, so Isaac bought it with the last of the money on his card and his mother got a bank statement and saw that he was still alive, so she texted him, *I'm sorry, I'm sorry, just please tell me where you hid your father's body*, but Saul saw the messages and made Isaac throw out the shitty old flip phone. Saul had been drunk then. Saul was only mean like that when he was drunk, and he hadn't been drunk for a week now, so things were almost fine.

"Pray for them," Saul says, louder this time. "Please."

Isaac shuffles to the kitchen, where the family of four is in five pieces and the air tastes of copper and shit. Most of the family has their guts on the outside, but Isaac doesn't count that as "separate pieces" in the same way that, in some country overseas, you can't declare a decapitated body dead at the scene unless the head is more than one hundred centimetres away. The only body in "separate pieces" is the daughter. Wait, no. A child of some kind. Isaac should know better. If he keeps thinking like that, one day Saul will kill him and the authorities will take one look at his corpse and mark him down as FEMALE, DECEASED and death will strip him of the one thing Saul allowed him to keep.

"What do you want me to say?" Isaac asks.

"I don't know," Saul says. "Anything."

So Isaac kneels, careful to find a spot where the blood won't stain his knees. He recites the prayer of St. Francis of Assisi. It's not one of his favourites but it gets the job done and it feels fitting, somehow.

"Do it again," Saul says, when Isaac finishes.

"What?"

"Again. Please."

Isaac does as he's told. Saul comes up behind him, eyes wide and boots squeaking on the waxed floors, and Isaac wonders if this is how his namesake felt when he walked with Abraham up the mountain, slowly realising his father hadn't brought a sacrifice to the altar—just a length of rope and a blade and him.

Isaac tries to sleep in the back of the car as Saul drives to the motel. It doesn't work, so when they check in, he pulls off his sports bra (without taking off his shirt; he always feels Saul's eyes on his back, waiting for a strip of pale bare skin to slip free) and collapses onto his side of the bed. It's been a while since he's slept in an actual bed. Saul brushes his teeth and scrapes blood from under his nails and his shadow moves in the strip of light spilling under the bathroom door.

No vodka. No drinking. Good.

Saul comes to bed. They don't touch, which is also good. The idea of Saul *on* him makes Isaac think of Saul *inside* him and his guts turn hot with fear, like they're trying to fever themselves out of him. No— stop thinking about that. He doesn't have a reason to be worried. Saul doesn't want to fuck him. Saul doesn't fuck men.

Nobody gives a shit what you call yourself. You have a womb. You bleed. A child could get milk from your body. Dad's breath singes the shell of his ear. *You're just sick. You're just confused. We can fix that.*

Isaac stays frozen like that, staring at the ceiling, for what feels like forever, but before Dad can shove fingers in his mouth or jam his tongue down his throat, Saul wakes in a fit, begging for a prayer. Isaac fetches Saul a glass of water and sits with him, walking him through the words. It distracts him from the half-bottle of acid in his bag.

"I can't get it," Saul whimpers. "I can't say it right."

"You've got the words down," Isaac assures him.

Acid looks *enough* like water. If he plugged his nose he wouldn't notice anything was wrong until it started to eat through his tongue and throat and slowly trickled down to burn out his internal organs. It'd just be swallowing hellfire. Or maybe he could cut a hole right below his belly and pour it right where it mattered. *That* would keep him from carrying a child. *That* would shut Dad up.

Saul kills another family a few days later, a few states over, this one a young couple with a baby. Isaac can't step into the nursery until Saul guides him with a hand on his lower back.

When Isaac prays, Saul sits in and listens. It makes Isaac stumble over his words. He says the Lord's Prayer because that one is muscle memory; he doesn't have to think about it too much, he can't think with Saul watching the arc of his back and the white curve of his neck like this.

"Again," Saul says. "It didn't work."

Isaac says it again. This time, Saul tries to follow along. *Our Father who art in Heaven—*

"Again."

Hallowed be thy name—

Saul presses the heels of his hands into his eyes. "Again."

Thy kingdom come—

"Please, please, again."

The dead man's throat is cut so deep Isaac can see the black and fatty yellow of his insides. Isaac rearranges the curve of the eyebrows and the pink of the lips until the man looks like the photo on the mantle back home. It's Dad on the bedroom floor now, turning the carpet red, staring up at the ceiling as if trying to figure out what the hell Isaac is praying to. As if he's suddenly doubted his belief and died knowing there will be nothing for him on the other side.

It's late but Saul won't risk a motel while they're still in Michigan so they're driving again. Isaac wants to sleep, but every time he closes his eyes, Dad is in the back seat with him, his face inches away and breath like maggot-pocked meat where prayers rotted in his gullet. It makes the spot under Isaac's belly burn like he'd already poured the acid down. Invisible hands hover around his neck, fingers spelling out *God made you a woman and if you have to choke that down then fucking choke*. A palm on the flat, scarred plane of his belly, where that fucking demon slept even after he'd starved himself to bones and swallowed bleach to get it out of him. He'd bled on the bathroom floor and pushed red, dying flesh out of him, but now it was biding its time, furious and waiting. *I hope it wakes up. I hope it kills you.*

Their first kiss is in the back seat of Saul's grey four-door, in the lot of a Methodist church at night, Isaac's hands trembling and his eyes squeezed shut and Saul softly holding his jaw like it might turn to dust between his fingers.

It's been four weeks, maybe. Isaac stopped keeping track of time because it doesn't matter, not really. Radio stations chirp about a roving killer and he gets sick when he sees cop cars in the rearview mirror. There was a DUI checkpoint a few days ago when they were crossing state lines and Saul had to pull over to let Isaac puke. But it's fine. It's better now. It's better than it ever was at home.

The kiss is Saul's idea. Isaac doesn't know if he wants it or not, but what he *does* want is to overwrite the sick taste in his mouth he's been holding for years, and right now this seems like the same thing. So he whispers, "Yes."

The kiss is almost… good.

Saul is broad and solid like something unliving, and when Isaac wraps his arms around his shoulders, jealousy creeps through him like the acid creeps up his fingers when he sleeps. His flannel jacket is rough under Isaac's hands and his hair is thick and soft and nothing like Dad's. It's not *almost* good. It's the closest to good he's ever gotten.

Saul wants to touch. Not just with his hands, with *everything*, pushing Isaac's shirt up to trail a line of kisses down his stomach, the same line hunters use to gut deer. Isaac draws other kinds of lines across his body and makes sure they're just as clear as if he had drawn them with a knife. This is where touch might feel fine, or at least where he can survive it. This is where touch will make him want to kill himself, where he will feel that parasitic demon fucking thing waking up in his stomach.

With lines like these, Saul can never put something inside of him.

"I didn't know you were into guys," Isaac says, fighting for air afterwards.

Saul replies, "We should sleep."

*

The next time Isaac prays, the Act of Contrition comes out. *I detest all my sins because of Thy just punishment, but most of all because they offend Thee, my God*—and Saul is fascinated by the lilt of the words and demands Isaac say it over and over until they both have it carved into the insides of their skulls. Once, Saul tries to say it alone, but once he reaches the end he clenches his fists and coughs in rage and says, "It didn't fucking *work*."

This new man looks even more like Isaac's father, but maybe that's because half of his face is a formless mash of red meat and white, slick bone. Isaac wonders if the blood would taste like holy water would taste like acid. When he wonders aloud, Saul gets some of it on his finger and wrenches Isaac's mouth open and smears it down his tongue. Tears spring to Isaac's eyes. Saul says, "Good." He kisses him. "Again."

Saul still feels like Abraham, but only a bit.

They have to sleep in the car again.

"Saul?" Isaac asks that night. His face is tucked into Saul's neck. It's safe here. His body is covered in bruises but he likes the ache and they distract him from the heavy, bulbous way his chest feels under Saul's oversized shirt. "Can I ask a question?"

"Anything," Saul whispers against Isaac's shoulder.

"What do you need me for?"

"You make sure God knows I'm doing this for Him." His hands curl in Isaac's hair, holding him close, eyes wide—child-like in his belief, his stubbornness. "I've never been able to talk to Him. But you can." His smile wavers, something struggling underneath. "I need you."

Isaac wakes up the next morning sore; an odd taste in his mouth.

Dad presses close to Isaac in the backseat, reeking of death and that blood on his tongue, and Isaac smothers a croaking noise behind his hand. It's late. The highway flickers by, their car hidden in the quiet of night, and Saul is groggy in the driver's seat. He takes a turn too tight and Isaac's stomach tries to force itself out of his mouth.

"Everything alright back there?" Saul asks. Isaac gulps down air.

"I don't feel good," he whispers. "Can we stay in a motel tonight?"

Saul looks at him warily in the rearview mirror.

They—Saul, really, Saul is the one with the money—book a room on the outskirts of a city, a place where the lights buzz and the TVs only get two channels. Isaac missed air conditioning and blankets and running water that doesn't come from a gas station bathroom, but right now all he can think about is throwing up. Isaac heaves at the door and Saul holds him upright.

"Alright," Saul murmurs. "Alright."

Isaac sits on the bathroom floor, pressing his forehead against the tiles before clamouring for the toilet and vomiting. Saul swears. The puke is hot and sour and tastes the way acid smells, the way he imagines it would taste—strong and choking and clinging to the tongue. His throat burns and his stomach cramps like someone has reached under his skin and squeezed it tight. Saul sits against the bathtub with him and rubs his back.

But Saul leaves to sleep eventually and Isaac strips off his shirt and pants and kneels on the floor in just his sports bra and boxers, his skin almost yellow in the dusty light. There's nothing left in his stomach to bring up. He crawls up to the sink and takes a desperate gulp of water from the faucet, little streams dripping over his chin.

He's felt like this before. It comes—cloudy at first, then ice-cold and clear, and he retches into the sink, clutching the counter and gasping for air.

Not again. He muffles a scream against his palm and bites down, hard.

Not again.

It's awake *it's awake IT'S AWAKE NO NO NO NO NO*

Saul digs the bottle of vodka out from the trunk of the car and goes out to the front desk to buy a week's worth of time. They were supposed to make their money last.

"You're going to get us caught," Saul accuses, the first cruel words he's said in so goddamn long.

Isaac doesn't care. Saul broke the lines. Saul can go fuck himself.

There's a swelling below Isaac's stomach when he sneaks out of the motel room at two in the morning. He takes five dollars in cash from Saul's wallet, the motel room key, and the flannel jacket that's too big on him.

There's a 24-hour dollar store across the street with crane flies gathering around the buzzing, half-broken sign. A bell jingles above the door when he opens it, and the sleepy employee at the door sits up to look at him.

"Evening," she says. "Or is it morning?"

Isaac finds what he's looking for in the back, hidden with the novelty items. Shot glasses—real glass, all different colours. Isaac stares at them for a moment as if the design actually matters, and he finally picks two. Clear, plain, simple. They clink a little too loudly when he picks them up and he winces.

He brings them to the register.

"This gonna be it?" the cashier asks sweetly.

Isaac grabs a chocolate bar. "This, too."

She rings them up without looking at them. She's looking at Isaac instead.

"Everything alright?" she asks.

"Yeah. Just tired."

She puts the cups in the bag and gestures to her own neck. "You've got—a little something."

Probably a bruise. Probably Saul. "I know."

When she finishes scanning his things, he hands over the cash, but she refuses to hand over the bag. Isaac stares at her.

"I have a cell phone in the break room," the cashier says quietly. "I've been where you are, sweetheart, a lot of girls have." Isaac makes a sound of disgust. *Girl.* "If you need someone to talk to—"

Isaac says, "Give me the fucking bag."

She does. Isaac eats the chocolate bar on the way back to the motel.

*

"What are you looking at?" Saul asks when he catches Isaac staring in the bathroom mirror. "Is something wrong?"

"No. I'm okay."

Saul frowns and comes forward to feel Isaac's forehead. His look of worry carves itself deeper and Isaac doesn't know how to feel. Vodka and kindness don't mix. Saul doesn't work like that. The *world* doesn't work like that. "You're warm," Saul says. "You should rest."

He lays down and Saul gets into bed with him, pulling the covers up over their shoulders. Saul's bare chest makes a better pillow than the too-soft, stale cushions. Vodka smells like sticking a permanent marker up your nose. Isaac buries his face in Saul's skin and it's not as bad.

"I've tried," Saul whispers eventually, lips pressed to Isaac's hair. "I've tried to pray. He doesn't want to listen to me."

What makes you think He listens to me?

"It's not like He talks back," Isaac manages.

"I *know*." Saul's body trembles like something possessed. "But I wasn't raised like you. I didn't grow up with Him. I don't understand."

You don't want to grow up the way I did.

You know what you saved me from.

Saul whispers, "Help me understand."

If Saul understands, he won't need Isaac anymore. FEMALE, DECEASED. Isaac is an extra mouth, a liability, just a tether to God and a warm body in bed.

How much is a warm body worth when it's a body like his?

"You never feel it," Isaac says. He tells the truth. It burns. "You never feel anything. You never will." Belief is screaming into a void that will never give a shit about you. It is knowing a man will kill you one day and kissing him anyway. "That's faith."

Saul keeps the vodka in the bathroom. Isaac sits on the floor again, mouth sour, staring at the half-empty bottle in his hands and the fingers turning white around it. He's never tried alcohol. Never wanted to. Never understood the point of drinking something that takes your body away from you when it was so hard to get it in the first place.

But.

This stuff burns, right? It burns going down?

Saul is out. Doing what, Isaac doesn't know. He threw up again this morning and Saul wanted him to stay in bed. He promised he'd be back soon.

Isaac puts the vodka back. He sets the shot glasses under the sink. After mulling it over for a second, he puts the acid up there, too. His fingers sting with the memory, the burning sliding up his veins, seeking out the heart, covetous.

The thing in his stomach cramps and moves. It's been just days and the fucking thing is already *moving*.

This is Saul's fault.

The door to the motel room makes a creaking noise as it opens, a flicker of warmth cutting through the artificial cold of the A/C unit. Isaac stumbles to his feet and wraps up in his sweatshirt again.

"Isaac?" Saul calls.

Isaac steps out of the bathroom. "Here."

Saul is smiling.

His eyes are wide and bright, gleaming with tears. He crosses the room in three massive strides and pulls Isaac into his arms, pressing kisses to his temple and cheeks.

"God bless you," Saul whispers. "God, God." He laughs, and it is a true, genuine laugh. Isaac's head spins. He's never heard that before. His body is limp in Saul's arms, unresisting. "You perfect thing."

When Isaac breathes, it's like something is squeezing his chest, refusing to let him get all the air in. "What happened?"

"*You were right.*" Saul holds Isaac's face in his hands, pressing their foreheads together. "You were right, I hadn't understood." He kisses him again, deep and grasping, a kiss of real *love*. "I had been so faithless. I had been so wrong."

"You—"

"How terrible of me to think I *deserved* to hear His voice." When Saul finally pulls away, he is practically sparkling with excitement, with clarity. Blood flakes off his fingers. "I—I was so selfish, thinking I deserved to hear Him just because I do as He wants. But I get it. I just need to trust Him. I trust Him." His smile is so wide it looks like his face might crack right in half. "Thank you. Thank you."

Saul doesn't need Isaac anymore.

His warm body isn't worth anything.

He is dead weight.

"I knew you could do it," Isaac whispers, forcing a smile. Saul has no need for a broken, disgusting thing like him. Not with a third on the way.

And Isaac has no need for someone who broke the fucking lines.

"You know what," Isaac says, "why don't we celebrate? Go sit." He reaches up to press a trembling kiss to Saul's slick cheek. "I'll get something for us."

Isaac doesn't have a choice. Never has. Never will. But at the very least, he can make sure *he's* the one that does it.

In the bathroom:

The first shot glass gets vodka.

Half the second glass gets acid.

The acid smells. He pours the vodka over top—it'll go down easier mixed with alcohol. Make it harder to stop once the tongue realises what it is.

It sizzles and hisses for a moment and Isaac's stomach sinks. What is it doing? Part of it bubbles and a little hiss of steam rises out of the cup.

But after a moment, it quiets. The liquids lay still. Isaac leans down to smell it and it doesn't smell like acid at all. Just vodka. Just marker. It's fine.

It's fine.

Isaac brings the cups out to the bedroom and pushes one into Saul's large, outstretched hand. Both cups are the same colour. Isaac stares at his own for a second, unsure. Saul is too drunk on God to notice.

"A toast," Isaac says.

Saul raises his glass. "A toast!"

Isaac downs his cup. Saul does, too.

It burns.

ANDREW JOSEPH WHITE is a queer, trans author and graduate student in George Mason University's Creative Writing program. His work has been featured in Transcendent 4: The Year's Best Transgender-Themed Speculative Fiction, *and* Twisted Anatomy: A SF&S Body Horror Anthology. *Find him at andrewjosephwhite.com or on Twitter: @AJWhiteAuthor.*

THE HOUSE BY THE SEA

Allison Floyd

"Far worse to be love's lover than the lover that love has scorned."
—*Nick Cave, "I Let Love In"*

Three Ways it Could have Happened

I.

Once upon a time, there was a woman. She was quite self-sufficient. One day, she met a man who made her realise there was a wound in her heart where love should be. But he was married! So that was out of the question.

THE END

II.

I was named for a drowned girl.

We both have literary names, followed by surnames that serve as the equivalent of the colour beige:

Ophelia Jones and Fitzgerald Smith.

We have a connection, you and me.

It's unspoken; no words are required.

I grew up in a cocoon lined with sharp things, but also lined with love. It was small and there was never enough air. It was warm and cosy. It jabbed and it hurt. It laughed and it loved.

It was confusing.

It was home.

You grew up in The Way and The Truth and The Light.

Then, one day, God stopped returning your calls.

It was a bad connection; there was too much static.

So we, each of us, were walking around with heart-wounds, with wound-hearts, two jagged puzzle pieces looking for the heart-pulp that would align with our own.

We met in the house by the sea.

You left; I did not.

There are several reasons this might be.

III.

I was holding the carafe, the dregs of coffee and grinds muddying the bottom, en route to the kitchen sink.

You were not a coffee drinker; you lacked the taste for bitter things.

I was explaining to you about my insomnia, the way it rendered my days a foggy, snarly blur.

"What specifically can I do to support you?" you asked, in that well-intentioned but clinical way you have.

"You can go upstairs and have a good rest of your day." It came out barbed; that wasn't my intention. Insomnia.

You receded like the waves outside the window, having found my sand too strewn with sharp rocks.

After I'd rinsed the carafe, I made my way upstairs. I felt you behind me, keeping a safe distance, as if I were a wounded animal, or a roaring fire. You didn't want to get bitten or burned.

This moment, small and unremarkable, snares me, snags my memory. Why?

Because: I wondered then—as I wonder now—if I found a way to properly contain myself, smooth the rough edges and render the dazzling undertows into placid pools, tear the storm clouds from the sky and paste a big yellow sun up there in their stead, would I have passed? Or would you still have found me wanting?

I wanted to tell you, always: "You're so beautiful, it's fucking lacerating."

But seeing as we were both boarders in the house by the sea— nothing more, and you with a family to return to once your business in town had concluded—that was out of bounds.

Also, you seem the sort to take a dim view of profanity.

Which is a fucking shame.

Also, you were kind, deeply and democratically so, and I watched the other boarders and the landlady—Mrs Hobbes, before she and you and the others all took your leave of this place, leaving me to haunt it like a hungry ghost—lap up the crumbs of your kindness like starving dogs. I felt myself doing the same. It shamed me. But if you've gone hungry your whole life, and then a gentle hand extends a crust of bread in your general direction, well, all bets are off.

It doesn't matter if it's nothing personal.

IV. (A BONUS!)

The nature of the problem is thus:

You: Please pass the salt.

Me: I have iodine deficiency!

You: We live by the sea and you cry a lot.

Me: And still I want for salt.

You: Please be sensible.

Me: I will not!

You: What specifically can I do to support you?

Me: Do you even have blood in your veins?

This house is drafty, made of old wood. The wind whispers through the rafters and the walls crack.

I think I might crack.

I walk up the creaky stairs and stare out the picture window on the second floor. The waves crash against the rocks, pummelling their will against the jagged edges.

I was the waves; you were the rocks.

The front door is locked.

If you could get out, then you can come back in.

But I can never leave.

In a rare moment of candour—perhaps it was the wine we shared fireside in the parlour one wintry evening when the sea outside raged as if to drown the world—you told me that you were born in the Philippines, to missionary parents. You had attended seminary school, and left when you realised, in so many words, that God was a point of view and there were infinite ways of seeing, many of which had led, throughout the ages, to horrific things.

The first invitation to leave the house by the sea presented itself in the form of two earnest evangelicals who showed up at the front door, brimming with invitations to join the congregants that Sunday, in celebration of their lord and saviour.

The way you listen so intently, it makes people turn their faces toward you as toward the sun, basking in the warmth and light—so rare, so very rare—of being truly heard, sincerely beheld.

You took their literature, in that warm but reserved way you have about you, and thanked them both—a young man and a young woman—profusely. If there were hints of strain in the way the ridges in your forehead deepened, in the way your tongue darted between your lips (something you always do, Fitz, when you are nervous), then I doubt that anyone watching you less intently than I do observed it.

I also doubt very much that anyone watches you as intently as I do.

You closed the door afterward, forgetting to lock it, and informed me—always hovering in your midst, just another moth starved for heat and light, just another lost soul aching to be heard and beheld—

that you would regretfully need to decline this invitation. You placed the literature in the fire, gently, almost reverently, issued a barely perceptible sigh, excused yourself, and trudged upstairs. (I almost said, "repaired to your chambers," like some stodgy Victorian. This is an old house; sometimes it feels like it's speaking through ne.)

I locked the door after you left. If you had no intention of leaving, then neither did I.

The way you slyly flirt and withhold is such a turn-on, more an insinuation, a whisper of flirtation, there and then not, the way the sea recedes from the shore outside these wide expanses of windows. Did it ever even happen, or have I misperceived? Are these just the desperate and starved imaginings of a lonely woman? Wondering as much is part of the allure.

Memories from the early days of our acquaintance, when this house had multiple boarders, before it became mine and mine alone, my prison and my sanctuary:

That time I arrived in the dining room, to find you already seated at the scarred wooden table, my mind on the matter at hand, the way I launched right into it—"I wonder—"

You looked up, smiled in that warm yet reserved way of yours. I felt suddenly acutely aware of the fact that I had dispensed with the preliminary social niceties.

I decided to start again. "How are you?"

You looked back down at the table, still smiling, said in your teasing way, "You wonder about me, Ophelia?"

I felt myself flush as I took my seat.

Outside, the sea was placid—perhaps deceptively so. Perhaps like you.

On another occasion, when I'd adjourned with my laptop to the dark, dimly lit library, hoping to find a peaceful place to work:

The way you wandered in shortly thereafter with your own laptop and took a seat behind me, silent, your presence as palpable as the leather-bound books surrounding us.

In our time together, it wasn't at all unusual for you to be lurking in the background, silent, gliding, like a shark encroaching upon its prey (I wish. Oh, to be your prey!). Frequently, you would take a seat behind me.

I looked at you and said hello. It seemed the thing to do.

"Ophelia," you said, your voice low, resonant, the way I imagine a cello would sound if given human form. "May I share this space with you?"

"Please do," I said. "Thank you for sharing this space with me."

You, under your breath: "That's lovely."

The way you hissed it.

The silence between us as we tapped away.

When I arose and bade you good evening (there I go again, with these archaic turns of phrase, more and more they come naturally), you looked up, your grey eyes intense, fathomless, unknowable, like the stormy sea outside.

"Ophelia," you said, "I wish the same for you."

You, a modern day Mr Rochester, a sparkling wish fulfilment fantasy, the way you dazzle and flash, but subtly, like a calm sea on an overcast day. You, the puzzle who rewards those who pay attention. You, so perfect that I sometimes wonder if I made you up in my head.

The second invitation to leave the house by the sea arrived in the form of a door-to-door drape salesman. Who knew there was such a thing? But, evidently, there is.

He carried in his portmanteau many fine fabric swatches: luxurious brocades, rich velvets, thickest linen, damask, silk.

I ran my fingers through them all; I couldn't help it.

The salesman interpreted my gesture as a sign of hope.

"Surely a drafty house like this could use some fine drapes to ward off the chill of the sea air," he said. "Come to town, visit our store, run your hands through our fine fabrics. There are many more to choose from."

I was brushing my fingers across a swatch of purple velvet when you emerged from the shadows and took your place behind me, your face alight with amusement.

I released the swatch. "I suppose the aubergine is a bit much?"

You smiled that wry smile of yours. "I thought all girls liked purple."

I blushed at the idea of myself as a mere girl.

And just like you, Fitz, to opt for the more prosaic "purple" over "aubergine". Not one for gilded or British affectations, you.

But surely even the most prosaic life requires a bit of poetry?

Surely even the most domesticated of dogs recalls—when the moon is full and the air crackles with the electricity of a coming storm and the black, wild night beckons—his wolf lineage?

Surely even a slightly wilting flower—a little worse for rough weather—still has thorns to snare the unwary, or the lovelorn?

I asked the salesman for his card. It was thick, printed on excellent cardstock.

Perhaps some day I shall venture into town, and run my hands through the fine fabrics: embrace the true and tangible things of this world.

After all, the house by the sea gets awfully drafty.

As does a life without poetry.

I could leave this house. I could do as you did—walk out the door and rejoin the world, or dash myself on the rocks below, an offering to the raging sea.

I could do this, but you put a spell on me.

You showed me my desire, long dormant, and reflected it back at me, until it grew roots and bound me to the spot.

And then, when you had assured yourself that I was well and truly planted, you told me of your intent to leave, to return to your family.

I reached for you then, snaking tendrils in an attempt to wrap around you, to keep you here. Look, said the tendrils, I am clever, and sensitive, and observant, like you. I am quick-witted and diligent and a hard worker, just like you. I have even—one needy, scraggly tendril whispered—in the right light, under the correct circumstances, even sometimes, been called beautiful.

Let me continue to intrigue you, to draw you in, that you may also take root here with me, that we might become part of the foundation of this house, and never leave,

never leave—

Never. Leave.

Let us stand still together while, outside, our constant companion, the sea, rages and calms itself, and rages again.

You dodged my tendrils easily, closed the door softly behind you, leaving so seamlessly that I wondered if you'd ever been there.

The third invitation to leave the house by the sea materialised in the form of the woman who watered the houseplants, before payment for her services ceased to materialise.

Shortly after you left, Fitz, and after everyone else had taken their leave of this place, the Lady of the Plants (as I like to think of her) paid a visit, battered aluminium watering can and plant food in tow. She failed to close the door firmly enough for it to remain closed, and soon the breeze had pried it open, left it ajar.

I hovered on the stairway, beholding the world outside—the wide expanse of sky, the seagulls circling, and, through the grove of cypress trees, the waves crashing on the rocks.

I beheld the world outside and I knew—this was my chance to rejoin it. To feel the wind on my face, to smell the salt air, to wander the cypress grove and listen to the sounds of the sea.

I made my way toward the bottom of the stairs, toward the door, toward the glorious world outside—

And found myself firmly rooted to the spot. Those vicious, snaking, invisible tendrils had wended their way between the floorboards and taken hold of my ankles, claimed me as their captive with their vicious grip.

I opened my mouth to scream, but no sound came out.

The wind, however, kindly obliged me and howled, a banshee keen.

Do you know—

I have never in my life felt so rigorously watched, observed, scrutinised, *seen*—as when you laid eyes upon me. And upon me. And upon me.

You were always hovering in the background, watching— watching me ladle soup, watching me fold clothes, watching me watching. I am a watcher myself, you see. Accustomed to watching, and not accustomed to being watched. It felt like a power dynamic upended, like a violation of sorts.

Is this what it is to be watched? Is this what those I've watched have been made to feel?

The idea displeases me.

Although—there is a thrill in being watched. In being deemed worthy of watching. I found myself performing for you. I made myself bright, showy, and shrill. I exaggerated my gestures; I raised my voice. I laughed as if it was I who had discovered mirth. I honed my wit until it could effortlessly halve a cantaloupe in one fell swoop. I mustered bravado, walked with a swagger, kept my posture ramrod straight. I watched intently, listened keenly, that you, the watcher, might recognise me as such.

We are kin, you and I, one and the same—two watchers watching in a world where everyone wants so badly to be watched.

Wants it so badly they can't see a damn thing.

Just two watchers, we, watching the world wring its hands, writhe toward the spotlight. We, two wraiths, very much of the flesh.

Quiet-not-quiet, I call it. Loud Quiet. The sort of quiet that's not quiet at all.

It's always the quiet ones.

A cliché rendered true by repeat occurrence—as with every other cliché.

How often do two watchers find one another?

I imagine it's rare.

But perhaps I flatter myself.

After all, even a watcher gets things in her eye—an itinerant eyelash obstructs the vision, a sharp shard of want.

Even a watcher, from time to time, blinks.

The fourth invitation to leave the house by the sea arrived in the form of a travelling purveyor of eyeglasses. He crossed the threshold into the foyer—the Lady of the Plants had left the door unlocked—opened his briefcase, and carefully laid out his wares: frames in every conceivable shape and colour, cat's-eye, round, half-moons, thick, chunky squares, and svelte rectangles; fire engine red, teal, every persuasion of black, grey, and brown, and patterns, even—leopard print, zebra print, polka dots, stripes.

"Come visit our office in town and we will fit you for a fine pair of spectacles," he said.

My eyesight has always been keen (I am, after all, a watcher), but the frames glistened and beckoned, shiny, bold, new.

I reached for a pair of cat's-eye frames, speckled in the corners with rhinestones. I wondered, idly, if they'd be too dramatic on my pale skin—I'd always been fair, but lately I was almost translucent, as if I were fading, barely there.

My fingers failed to grasp them. It was almost as if, dear reader, they passed through the spectacles, were such a thing possible.

I reached for them again, to similar (lack of) results.

I glanced up at the salesman, arranging my face into an expression of sheepish apology.

He himself was looking rather pale as he hastily gathered his wares back into his briefcase.

"Wait!" I said. "I'd like to try these frames!"

The salesman—a spectacle himself at this point—opened his mouth, closed it, and opened it again, like a beached goldfish gasping for air.

He slammed his briefcase shut and tripped over his feet as he bolted for the door.

I hurried after him, but he slammed the door shut, and I couldn't for the life of me get the damn thing open.

It was, all in all, a vexing encounter.

Even a watcher, from time to time, blinks.

Sometimes I feel that this house is watching me, the way you so intently watched me, eyes lingering on my most mundane gestures, rendering them something unspeakably private. I gaze out of the floor-to-ceiling windows in the parlour, and feel my gaze returned. I peruse the spines of the leather-bound books in the library, and feel myself perused. I traverse the creaky stairs, and the groaning wood speaks to me with the force of a verdict rendered. Even the wind is sentient, the way it rattles the windowpanes, insistent fingers rapping the glass, demanding to be let inside. The way the sea itself would swallow me if it could cross this threshold.

Or if this threshold would let me cross it.

I remember the day you crossed this threshold, to be swallowed by the world, to be swallowed by your life.

The day you averted your gaze.

The day you said, "My business here is concluded. I must return to my family."

The day I died inside.

I was so civil, cordial even. Cool, calm, collected, like the sea on a still day.

"I see," I said.

"Safe travels," I said.

"All the best to you," I said, and you could have served my tone of voice with crustless cucumber sandwiches.

I've come to think of this house as my captor and my keeper. Its weathered wood cradles me, coddles me, shelters me from the violence and the cruelty of the elements outside. It shrouds me, enshrines and ensnares me, precludes me from joining the land of the living—much like that old, dark cocoon of my chrysalis days. And now I, a tattered butterfly with bent wisps for wings—beating against the glass at a world that will not grant me entry.

After you'd gathered your effects, you pressed a letter in my palm. The envelope was cream-coloured, the paper cold and crisp—much like you.

"Open this when I'm gone," you said. It wasn't a request.

And then you left.

I remember tearing the envelope open, slicing my finger against its edge in the process, the bright red blood drops blossoming on the wooden floor.

I remember ascending the stairs.

I remember my bare feet on the cold black-and-white tiles of the bathroom, as if the floor wished to draw all the warmth from my body. Turning the taps of the claw-foot tub.

I remember drawing a bath.

I remember the will to drown.

I remember the raging of the sea.

Much time passed (how much? How does one quantify the vastness of the ocean?) in the house by the sea: my cradle-grave, my captor-cocoon, my crypt-keeper.

And then—

One fateful day—

(as I always knew you would)—

You.

Came.

Back.

You came back!

Our reunion, alas, was not the blissful one I had anticipated.

You were not happy to see me.

You were not happy to see me, but I knew—

The house had returned you to me, tossed you upon my shore, the way the sea disgorges driftwood for which it has no further use, to line the shore like bones.

"Take me with you," I said.

You gripped the weathered banister to steady yourself.

You were in a bad way. Why, you even crossed yourself, in the Catholic way—your faith a phantom limb twinging, that which caused you greatest pain your only hope of comfort.

What is it, this anguish for God, for love, for holiness and wholeness?

For phantom limbs that twinge, for lost teeth, our tongues trailing the bloody wound where the tooth used to be?

Our tongues dared not trail more than that. And so we subsisted, like ghosts, on the crumbs of our want.

You crossed yourself, and you said to me, "You belong here. This is your home."

The wind whipped through this drafty old house, made its bones crack, made it moan its assent.

I knew you were right.

The house belonged to me, and I to it.

And then I knew—and then I said—

"If you won't take me with you, then I will take you with me."

The house shuddered then, a massive exhale.

Oh, Fitz—you always kept yourself so much to yourself. But in that moment—

You were mine.

The fifth invitation to leave the house by the sea arrived via a newspaper someone had left in the parlour before I became the house's sole tenant. It was the local section, splayed open, and I noticed at the bottom of a page, of all things, a coupon for caskets—courtesy of the Gentle Goodbyes Funeral Home (!).

Increasingly I suspect that that I'll only ever leave the house by the sea when I've shed my corporeal form.

In the spirit of being prepared (sooner or later, we all shed our corporeal forms), and in the spirit of being frugal (it was, dear reader, a twenty percent discount), I noted the phone number on the coupon and repaired to the kitchen to use the old rotary phone.

Everything is old in the house by the sea.

I reached for the receiver and—nothing.

It was as if my fingers failed to connect with it altogether.

I tried again, in vain.

I tried once more—vanity.

Vanity of vanities, all is vanity.

Why does nothing in this house ever seem to work?

Why does everything—even the simplest of things—evade my grasp?

Why, Fitz, did you?

It's a loop, an endless loop, as endless as the ocean—

Why won't you listen to me?

Why won't you come back?

And why can't I leave the house by the sea?

A memory crashes on the shore, dissipates like spume, comes rushing in again:

I fell asleep, I woke up, and everyone was gone.

I must have been out for some time.

I wandered the house looking for them—for you, most especially.

But no one was there.

It was lonely—the sounds of the sea, the hissing wind, the creaking lamentations of this old, warped wood, the arthritic architecture of this house, my only companions.

I remember—

I thought I should leave too. I made my way to the front door, turned the handle. It didn't budge. It was as if my hand went through it, made no impression upon the brass whatsoever. As if I were made of ether.

Of course, this wasn't possible. I tried again. And again, to the same result.

Which is to say, none.

This is an old house, set in its ways. For whatever reason, it was not of a mind to let me leave through the front door.

I wandered the house for what felt like a long time, then, tracing my fingers along various surfaces: windowsills, panes of glass, the scarred dining room table, the bannisters, the bathroom mirror. On none of these surfaces did I leave so much as a fingerprint.

Then, an idea—

I hurried into the kitchen, to the walk-in pantry, to the shelf where the flour was kept. My plan was to scatter it across a counter and see whether I could make fingerprints in the white powder. But I couldn't retrieve the cannister from the shelf, let alone open it.

I felt the panic overtake me with the violence of high tide.

Something was very, very wrong.

Who knows how long I spent in this limbo? The endless sense of flailing, sans limbs. The excruciating, interminable wait for—what?

I knew you'd come back.

You'd left something behind. Something important.

I knew you'd return for the letter you wrote me—the one that said simply, "It was a pleasure to burn."

We both knew what it meant.

Yours was a tender heart, after all, and furthermore we both knew that objects imbued with this kind of energy had power, power that could be misdirected, power that could lay waste and leave chaos in its wake if not properly contained. You weren't one to leave loose ends untied.

You came back for the letter.

The great, thundering joy I felt when I saw you striding up the walkway. The way the air itself became electric, alive.

I ran to greet you, to tell you everything I hadn't.

The look on your face, drained of all its colour—you looked as if you'd seen a ghost.

I opened my mouth to speak. "Fitz—"

"You aren't here."

You said it with the violence of an oath.

"You aren't here. You can't be."

I reached out for you then.

You recoiled as if stricken.

I knew if I could only find the right words, I could set things to right.

But the right words have always eluded me.

"Fitz—"

You backed away, toward the door, and I felt myself die all over again.

I had died, by my own hand, used them to open my wrists, and drowned like that, in the claw-foot tub, your letter beside it: an undoing, a binding, a talisman, a tattoo.

I saw it clearly now—I had sought to free myself from the prison of my skin and, in so doing, from the agony of desire.

And yet, here I was, ether, and no freer for it.

With a trembling hand, you opened the door.

The wail that escaped me was ungodly.

"Fitz, wait! I'll come with you!"

"That," you said, your deep voice quivering, sending shock waves through the drafty house, "is impossible. You don't exist. You can't. And if you do, you must remain here."

"No!" The house groaned with me, its bones shook with my rage. "I won't lose you again!"

You bolted then, slamming the door behind you. But it was too late, for now I knew.

I passed through the door as easily as the wind passes through clouds.

I see this part so clearly:

You are sprinting, you look behind, you run faster, you trip at the edge of the cliff.

I overtake you.

I channel the full force of everything I've ever felt for you, every last anguished moment of the exquisite pain of loving you. I am no longer embodied, but the fury of my feelings—it's stronger than ever. It rages like the sea when it's storming.

I loved you so much.

It was not enough.

And now I shall want no more.

With everything in me, I will myself into being, and I will my being to do my will. The wind wants for hands but can rip trees out by the roots. I make myself into the wind.

I rush into you.

Down, down we tumble, skidding across the rocks, those jagged sentinels watching over the sea.

Down we tumble into the sea itself. It swallows us as if to slake an ancient thirst.

Well, it swallows you.

And now I will always know where to find you.

You were never mine, any more than the sea.

But now we both belong to it.

I feel my hold relinquishing itself, feel what remains of me dispersing into the air like mist.

I've chosen not to drown again. The sea has laid its claim to me, but I have established the terms: I am a neighbour, and not a captive.

Perhaps I will now be as the wind.

Perhaps when my song rustles the cypress grove along the cliffs, a lovelorn woman, wandering, adrift, will cock her ear and heed my warning:

Yes, it was a pleasure to burn. But—

Better not to love at all than in vain.

ALLISON FLOYD's work has appeared on Defenestrationism.net, *the* Submittable *blog, and* On Spec Magazine, *among others. Her as-of-yet-unpublished novella,* Bluebeard's Bel Air Bachelor Pad, *reimagines* Rock of Love *in an even more ghastly light than the original. She currently lives and writes in her own private Idaho.*

ACKNOWLEDGEMENTS

When I first sent out the call for submissions for *Dark Hearts,* I thought I'd struggle to collect enough stories. By the time the deadline arrived, I'd received in the region of 650. I was absolutely blown away by the response, and I am grateful to every single writer who took the time to send their work. If only I'd had space for more.

Thank you so much to all of my lovely contributors, to Ashley Van Elswyk for the beautiful illustrations, Amanda McIlreavy Scott for the original cover design, and to everyone who lent their advice, support, and kindness during the production of this book. You are all stars!

Much love,

Antonia

COMING SOON FROM GHOST ORCHID PRESS

ghostorchidpress.com

www.ingramcontent.com/pod-product-compliance
Lightning Source LLC
Chambersburg PA
CBHW061603100726
47898CB00002B/507